THE UNORTHODOX OX

THE UNORTHODOX OX

THOMAS MORISON

EDITIONS ZORZAL
MONTRÉAL, QUÉBEC

Copyright © 2014 by Thomas Morison

All rights reserved.

No part of this book may be reproduced in any form or by any electronic or mechanical means including information storage and retrieval systems, without permission in writing from the author. The only exception is by a reviewer, who may quote short excerpts in a review.

This book is a work of fiction. Names, characters, places, and incidents either are products of the author's imagination or are used fictitiously. Any resemblance to actual persons, living or dead, events, or locales is entirely coincidental.

Cover design by anonymous contributor

Library and Archives Canada Cataloguing in Publication

Morison, Thomas, author
The unorthodox ox : a novel / by Thomas Morison.

Issued in print and electronic formats.

ISBN 978-0-9920750-4-0(pbk.).--ISBN 978-0-9920750-1-9(pdf)

I. Title.

PS8576.O6838U56 2014   C813'.54   C2014-905807-1
                                        C2014-900086-3

www.thomasmorison.com

First Edition: January 2014
Editions Zorzal

Printed in Canada

I

It was a pasture of grass. In the field cows were ruminating. He walked towards a fence.

— Then for the funeral it will be distressing to make the arrangements, he said.

He came to the fence. She set a glass down on a tree stump. He opened a gate. They stepped out into the field.

— Would you like to take a walk? she asked.

They walked off through the grass. The cows followed them. They came to a spot and stopped. They were far enough out into the field. The lights from her house were on off in the distance.

— And what happens when resigned to die? You give up and what happens? Is there a moment of reflection? Is there an epiphany? Or is it the same as what you would imagine? And we should hope that it's not as bad as the alternative, which might be to become a martyr, if that were an alternative.

— What alternative, to what? she asked.

— I don't know. I've no idea. I might be exaggerating a little. You can understand why, I would, he said.

— I understand, yes.

Then he took advantage of her understanding and he presented to her his expected marriage proposal.

— Yet this is maybe the wrong time, anyway, Karol, let's imagine we're lucky to be alive and we can make our promises to each other and marry one another, and I should never stop asking until asked to stop asking or until I've given you my soul and it's yours, and would you take my soul from me?

They walked on.

— Your soul would take my soul, he said.

She agreed to take his soul. The sun was coming up. The cows began to graze. They walked back to her house mourning in the

9

early mourning.

§

Then on the day of the funeral he asked to read to her the eulogy for his late mother.
— So you want to read the eulogy to me? she asked.
— If you'd like to lend an ear.
— When?
— Perhaps there is another time that would be preferable?
— Maybe another time would be better.
— But today is the funeral.
— All right, go ahead then.
— If you'd prefer that I didn't.
— Read it if you have to.

And having inconveniently interrupted her, he was to read her his eulogy.

— I didn't know. I don't know how to begin. *Today, we are sad. But let us find solace in looking back on what we will always have to remember her for. For how she knew how to charm us we will remember her. For the advice she freely offered us we will remember her. For how she listened to us and led us to understand our innumerable problems and those of others, we will remember her. And for those who knew her, we know how she reconciled the differences we had. She was able to turn enemies into friends without anyone realizing it before it was too late. And I think she got pleasure out of taking the pleasure of being angry at someone, she'd turn things around before there were problems. Though sometimes created problems where there weren't any, but we all do that. Yes, we worry, and what we're worrying about becomes the problem. And as for the worrying she did worry, and on that score we have ourselves to blame. But we shouldn't worry about having caused her to worry too much since she liked to listen to what anyone had to say. No problem was too small, nor too big, nothing was lost that couldn't be found. And nothing is lost if you know where to look for it, and nothing is lost if we look hard enough. But is it true that nothing is lost? When it happens that in the end our lives are lost. We die and lose everything and we can't come back to life to see what we could have done. Or maybe we do come back to life if we are remembered kindly by those we were kind to, by those we loved.*

He looked at her for her opinion.

— You're asking for criticism for your eulogy?

— I wouldn't have thought it would be so difficult to get right.

— I can't help you.

— I suppose not. I don't know why I asked.

— You thought you had to probably.

— So that maybe you wouldn't criticize me after the fact.

— I can tell you it is not perfect, Harold.

— You've no suggestions?

— Perhaps you might try being honest. She's dead after all, at least you can now be honest.

— You have a point, Karol, but what good would that do?

He worked on revising the eulogy and he delivered it at the funeral.

Then after the ceremony mourners expressed their appreciation for what had been said by him, and they gave thanks for the words spoken by the minister, who had given a formal eulogy that was personal; the pastor had been a friend of the family, he had known the deceased well.

On a dusty road they were heading off to the burial.

In the car when going to the cemetery and going over details for the burial the minister mentioned that the grave-side service was to be his last. He was to be a retired pastor. The last rites to perform was the end of a life's calling, and that was a lot to have to deal with he said to those riding in the car.

So at the grave-side following the burial and in conversation with the minister.

— Allow yourselves the time you need to grieve. It is important to allow yourselves the time to do so.

— Thank you, and for you to be retiring has to be sad or it is a relief? A cheque for the services we'll send to you.

— Let me send a bill first.

The minister wished them well.

The mourners were going out through the cemetery gates. From where cars were going by on the dirt road dust was rising and settling. It was quiet in the cemetery. The two of them were by the grave.

— I reminded him he was retiring and I felt bad for him, that's why I said I'd send a cheque to him.

— You were sympathizing with him as he was with you.

— Yes, it was considerate of him to say that we must grieve.

They walked down the cemetery lane. They read the names and dates on the monuments and headstones of acquaintances and of those anonymous.

— Poor us, who've been left behind and we don't know why, he said.

— You are asking me why? she asked.

— Not really. No.

They got through a period of grieving and it was sometime afterwards that they were ready to make their wedding plans and so regardless of their incompatibility, they were to marry one another, finally, and after having often reconsidered the idea many times before.

Then it was as they were making arrangements for their wedding reception party that they had not considered that it might have happened that too much could be drunk too quickly by too few. And a row broke out, having maybe to do with unresolved differences that there might have been. Then in the aftermath of the breakdown and the break-up of the reception party, and as they were disavowing the resulting damage, they wondered what had happened, how, why, who had said what.

— We might not have invited those who did not approve of us getting married, he said to her.

— We shouldn't have had an open bar. You think this is somehow amusing? she asked.

— You think we should have charged for the drinks?

— Are you going to ruin my life? Is that what you are going to do now?

— No, I'll ruin my own, because why else would we have got married?

— You would like me to pity you for this.

— No, I mean to be self-pitying. I was addressing myself out of self-pity. You might want to do the same.

She was rightfully and justifiably upset, incensed, and indignant.

The Unorthodox Ox

He was supposedly unmoved.
— What have I done? she asked.
— I ask myself the same question, Karol.
— What have we done?
— We should have asked that before.
— I thought we did.
They did not know who had asked what.

§

On his wedding night he was upstairs in their bedroom. He was sitting in front of a window in a chair. He was looking at his own reflection in the windowpanes that in the dark was an outline of a shadow of himself.

She eventually went upstairs into the bedroom.

He was watching her reflection in the windowpanes. She prepared herself for bed. She brushed her hair, her teeth, her skin, exfoliated herself as was her habit. She lay down onto her side of the bed. She turned off the light. He was sitting in darkness, and from his restlessness he got up and he went downstairs and he went outside and he climbed up to stand on one of two tree stumps in the yard. One tree stump was hers, the other was his. For the time he remained there, there was no call for him to get down and go inside. She was asleep.

In the morning they almost avoided confronting one another.

— About yesterday's significant problem, maybe today's problems, and perhaps tomorrow's problems.

— What do you want to say to me, Harold?

— That I'm going outside and if you want you can come running after me and ask me what my intentions are.

— What are your intentions? You can tell me what they are.

— No, you can come chasing after me and ask me what they are. Hound me until I tell you.

He ran out into the backyard, he walked past the stumps. He went out into the field.

She did not go after him and she left herself taking his car that had been blocking hers, and away she drove off on a road through fields of sunflowers and when she came out from between two fields, she saw him in the field he was walking off and away in. He saw she was driving away in his car. He stopped walking. She stopped driving. They looked at each other for a brief moment.

He went on across the open field. He was heading towards a river where at the banks he went along at the speed of the water that at the bends passed him by, cooling the air off.

The day was pleasant, the sun warm, but it began to rain. There was anvil lightning. The ambient electricity in the air stood his hair up on end. The river rose to nearly overflowing. The storm was too strong to be out in, yet it did not last. The sun came out. An arching rainbow appeared attaching itself at either end to fields of sunflowers. Then the momentary calm afterwards was interrupted by birds singing up their own storm, their calls he identified, distinguishing the song of the Eastern Wood Pewees from that of Black-throated Blue Warblers and the Yellow-throated Vireos from the Rose-breasted Grosbeaks and those from the songs of many other birds, and that is interesting, when the "what" is as important as the "why". Then why had there almost been a flood? Why had he been saved from it, if he had been saved and from what? Though for this kind of reckoning there are circumstances for which the choices there are to make will be regretted even when choosing to do nothing is the wise idea, and in what was to follow that might have been the choice to have selected.

He walked on through a field of mud, he got on to and was walking on a road. On the surface were worms that had come up from a ditch from along a cemetery. He was going along his way when from down the road, behind him, a car came. It drove quickly by and ahead of him it swerved to avoid running over a cat that also had come up from the ditch of the cemetery. The car slowed down, and it accelerated.

There was nothing he could have done to have helped the animal. Fur had been stripped off its back. From out of its hind end was hanging a length of uncoiled intestines.

He examined it. He assessed what the reactions of others would be. Would he provide details that he was making note of? Would anyone want to know them? There are those who do.

Then he would have preferred not to have involved himself and not to have notified the cat's owner. But there was no reason

The Unorthodox Ox

he knew of not to tell Miss Mary-Adeline MacSweeney, as she was not the sort of person who would have been suspicious. She was an artist, a musician, and it was to be expected that such a person would accept that a witness would report what he knew, and that it was a matter of him being in the wrong place at the wrong time.

Miss MacSweeney's house was nearby on the town limits. The cat may have been on its way home.

He removed the collar and he pushed the remains off the road into the ditch of the cemetery.

Then it was in spite of the circumstances, but not regardless of them that that afternoon he was scheduled to pick up an order of vegetables and fruits that he purchased from Mary-Adeline MacSweeney, he, being a customer, and the produce he bought from Miss MacSweeney included leafy greens and tuberous vegetables; she cultivated fruit trees and bushes of berries of which weather-sensitive varieties were housed in small tropical hot-houses. Then what she would have expected from his visit was for his order to be filled. She would greet him pleasantly.

He went down the road. He came to a line of trees that enclosed Mary-Adeline MacSweeney's property and protected the garden. He turned up a lane that led to her house, and through the trees he saw Miss MacSweeney in her garden standing between two hot-houses. She was surveying damage caused by the storm. She saw him and waved and she went into her house to soon come out and meet him at her door with his order of vegetables and fruits, saying hello with such joy, speaking as if for all there is to praise that grows under the sun. He would have wanted to have taken his order and gone off having said nothing.

She seeing that he was wet and muddy asked if he would like to hose himself off. He thought he would like to.

Mary-Adeline MacSweeney was fashionably dressed and it was noticeable that she was to be admired for her appearance and her kindness, her forthrightness, for a love for what was natural, for her talent as a musician, and for what was not an overstated sense of purpose.

He hosed himself off and he broke the news.

— It was quick. He didn't suffer for long.

He got out the collar and gave it to her. She held the collar up. A tiny bell on it tinkled. She paced back and forth on the front porch of her house. She said, "Sam, my Sam." Then she composed herself and she apologized for embarrassing him and herself. He made his apologies. They made reassurances for how it was unnecessary to excuse what was unfortunate.

He was getting cold standing in his wet clothes. She invited him inside.

It was later he was on the floor by a fire, and having drunk a little he had almost fallen asleep.

So to have lit a fire, to have talked, to have fallen to the floor, and to have continued on and ending up almost asleep beside each other from exhaustion. It should have been impossible. But there was no turning back from the decision to proceed, which would have meant having missed out on a possible missed opportunity.

But still, nevertheless, as the conversation was beginning to gather momentum and was moving along and charging ahead, there had been a point where it might have gone in a different direction, but Miss MacSweeney had taken the lead for them. He would not have presumed to have taken the initiative, he was following along, knowing that that was being asked of him. So she had told him stories about her cat, how she had come by him (he was a stray who had wandered into her life), there were the problems she had had with him as a kitten.

They talked about different subjects. She had made the drinks for them. Then she had said to him as they were sitting on the floor in front of the fire and looking into the flames that she felt that the world was going to hell. It looked like it. It was worrisome to imagine and see what was happening and to consider how unhappy people always were, and there was and is the pointlessness of the work that many have to do and there were and are always so many lives being squandered, and then, how so few have and have had the right to live decently and that the time that they were living in was not hopeful. She was speaking to him in a gentle voice and talking about what was familiar to him about the kind of sad issues that appealed to his sensibilities. And how grateful they were for the comfort they had offered one another. They were appreciative of the vitality of their actions that seemed to make up for all the impossible sadness there is in the world or so it seemed until it was

The Unorthodox Ox

over, and everything came rushing back. Then after another round of discussing universal disappointments, it had been too much to bear and they had drunk themselves into a mild stupor, which was when they had almost fallen half asleep, though they were awoken when a coal jumped from the fire and that had occupied them with the harmless burn he had sustained off to one side of his navel to which she had administered to with a cutting from an Aloe Vera plant, and that gesture, as it had showed concern, had convinced them to make the effort once again to ease their pain.

The fire was a bed of coals.

— Is your burn still burning? she asked him.

— Not too much, and this is the kind of agony that feels good to be thankful for.

— It will heal quickly. And would you like something to eat? You could put on some weight. Ten kilos wouldn't hurt you. You're skin and bones.

— Yes, I wish I could say I had some weight to lose.

— I can cook a supper for us, if you can stay for supper.

— I'd like to, but by now my wife will be expecting me. I'm afraid she'll be wondering where I am and what I'm up to. We were recently married. I won't tell you when as I would rather not give the wrong impression. So I am not an expert at keeping secrets and I'll have to see if I should be honest or lie to her. Might I ask what would you do if you were suddenly thrown into my situation?

— I'd wait to see what might be the best thing to do maybe.

— I could ask for forgiveness, but I will not be forgiven without an explanation. And I imagine, you, like me, are probably the one to forgive others?

— Forgive me if I have caused you a problem.

— No, it's nothing that I wouldn't have asked for in my wildest dreams.

— Are you hungry?

— Starving.

Then it was perhaps because he was not able to stay and share a meal with her that she compensated him as he was leaving with an extra large order of vegetables and fruits of which he would have been better off to have had less of, the quantity was more than he was able to carry easily, the height of the box she had given him made it difficult to see where he was going, but he couldn't have said, "No, no, it's too much."

He was walking away hungry with his arms full of food.

— We will see each other soon? he asked her hopefully.

— I hope so, too.

— Tomorrow?

— That'd be convenient. I have plans I can change. Tomorrow then, she said.

He was going along under the trees and down the streets between the houses of the town. A dog was barking.

At a bench in front of the town church (the church that was to be torn down), he stopped to rest and he sat on the bench. He looked up at the steeple, then he might have been wondering what in God's name for Christ's sake it was pointing at.

He got up and went along struggling with the load, but then, by discarding a few items as he went, he lightened it, as the box kept getting heavier.

§

He removed his clothes at the front door. The front light came on. A bicycle in the street went by in the dark. The door opened.

— Good evening, I took my clothes off not to wear them inside. I fell into some mud this afternoon.

— It's only me, Harold.

— How are you, Helen?

— Fine. I stopped by to tell you to make my daughter happy if you can.

And his mother-in-law said to him that had she met someone like him when she was young they would have made each other as happy as could be.

— I'd have felt the same way, he said.

— Karol asked me to say something to you, but all I can say is, don't take my example as one to follow.

— I shall try not to.

— So what a day it was. There was flooding.

— The storm came on quickly. I got caught out in it.

— Then she said she would come home late, and there's nothing

I can tell you other than that. It's already late. You work tomorrow. I'll let you get some sleep.

— I have to work, yes.

He accompanied her outside to see her off to her house that was a few houses away.

Then she said to him to be happy himself. He vouchsafed he would.

The box that he had set down on the stoop he picked up. He noticed it was lighter. He went inside with it and into the kitchen. He put away the produce.

He cleaned himself up and he went to bed and he was falling asleep as he was going over what he was worrying about a little as he was drifting off, which was not to have provided him with any moral comfort from what he woke up to.

She was standing over him and looking down at him. She was brushing her skin. He smiled up at her innocently enough.

— I was wondering, Harold, if I were to ask for you to brush yourself, that thick hide of yours? Because it's like getting in bed with a shedding snake. I've been thinking to ask you to. Or I might do it for you.

She threw back the covers.

— I was angry at you this morning. I can get angry just thinking about it, she said.

— You have a reason to be.

— And now I am bothering you, and it's usually you who is bothering me.

— I do.

— You do. You admit it. And I should tell you that I had a minor accident with your car. I wasn't hurt.

— As long as you weren't hurt.

— Do I look like it? And did you speak with my mother? She asked to say something to you.

— She told me to make you happy.

— Then make me happy and let me brush you. Look at you, covered in flaking skin.

She got him to get up out of the bed and had him remove what she said were his nightclothes and she brushed his arms, legs, back, and chest. His skin turned pink from her angry brushing. He had thought to cover his burn with the waistband of his underwear.

She finished with him and told him he was ready to go back to sleep. She lay down herself. She instructed him to have a good night's sleep.

But she had disturbed him, he was unable to get back to sleep. Then he got up to go down to the kitchen, and he ate two peaches of those that Mary-Adeline had given him, they were juicy and sweet. He restrained himself from eating a third peach, a large lump of ripe fruit, and it was as he was reflectively savouring the second peach that he was in a state and was fretting about whether or not there is any rest for those who worked high up in the office towers above the rooves of the shorter buildings where he spent his days at work.

The two peach pits when he was finished with them he discarded.

The third peach he had for breakfast. That was the end of them.

Then it was in the morning as he was leaving to go out the door to go to work that he told her what had happened on the road. Karol objected to his not having told her the night before.

— It was late to trouble you. I'll spare you the details, he said.
— How terrible.
— It was that.
— I always liked his occasional visits.
— That's why I thought I should tell you.
— How awful.
— So I shouldn't have told you?
— No, you should have.
— It was an unpleasant sight. I am sorry about it as well.

Then she suggested that she would like to pay Miss MacSweeney a visit to tell her how sorry she was. He countered her suggestion, and he argued that Miss MacSweeney would want to be left alone in her grief, as would be the case if it were themselves maybe.

— If it were us, Karol, we wouldn't want someone forcing herself on to us and to tell us how she knows how we must feel. If it were us, I mean.
— Are you looking to annoy me with such a comment?
— I have no right to annoy you.
— You have the right, don't abuse it.
— You don't know her well. It's just a cat.

The Unorthodox Ox

— Small considerations can make a difference.

— But it does not help to minimize what someone else is feeling. That might happen without you knowing it.

— That is not what I am going to do.

— It might happen. Why risk it?

— I am not going to risk anything.

She could pay a visit that morning. She had the time, she said.

Then he did not have a convincing or plausible nor an uncompromising argument that could have wholly dissuaded her.

— Then is there anything else that I should not forget to remind you of? That I have forgotten to tell you? Or that you can think of to tell me? she asked.

— No, I can't think of anything.

— Well, I can't either.

— There must not be then.

But he might have thought to have asked her about the accident she had had.

Then before he got into his car he looked it over; there was no visible damage, scratches or dents. Her accident could have had to do with mechanical failure, but there was not much he would have figured out for that. He was not knowledgeable of mechanical workings for how what is relied upon is designed. Although he knew that there are reasons for wanting to know why and how devices break down without warning, and that it can happen when hitting a top speed that a car, a plane, a hot-air balloon, will explode into millions of fragmented pieces, and for what there is to prevent this: faith. Then it was an act of faith on his part that allowed him to verify that there was nothing wrong with his car, and he roared off in it to go to work.

§

Mary-Adeline MacSweeney opened her door to Councillor Elrod who introduced himself, and the municipal councillor gave the reason for such an early intrusion. He excused the hour.

— I knew already, thank you, I thank you for coming to let me know, in any case, she said to him.

Then Councillor Elrod asked if she would like to have her cat's remains, or would she prefer for them to be delivered to a rendering plant for proper disposal, and so as he was the municipal councillor he knew the whereabouts of the rendering facilities. The bag with the remains in it that he had brought, he would take care of it, if she approved.

The offer for disposal of the remains she accepted, and the Councillor was explaining how and what he had found. Then he was ready to leave when Karol arrived, and she said she had come to say what she could.

— I'm very sorry, she said.

— Thank you. It happened quickly apparently. He was old. I suspect he was unable to get out of the way quickly enough, said Miss MacSweeney.

— It is a treacherous stretch of road for man and animal alike, said the Councillor.

— The poor creature, said Karol.

— It is tragic when our pets come to grief in such a horrific fashion, he stated.

Then Miss MacSweeney asked if she might serve them a refreshment to thank them for their trouble and kindness.

That was kind of her, he said, yet he was not able to stay for long. He had to rush off to work, he said as they were going inside. He left the bag by the outside door.

Miss MacSweeney invited them to take a seat when showing them into her living room, if they would. She excused herself to go and get what she would prepare to serve them. She would be right back, she assured them.

There was sunlight shining in through floor-to-ceiling windows and reflecting off of a white pine floor and over black leather furniture. The floor and dark furniture were in evident stark contrast to each other.

They sat down.

— We'll get hot sitting here before long. And so then people do drive fast down that road. They go whistling by the graveyard.

— In the bag?

— The remains.

— For God's sake.

— There are pet owners who want to bury their pets in their

The Unorthodox Ox

yard to have them close by. It is what a few do. I wouldn't do that myself.

— But who would?

— Some do. I can assure you of that as I can assure anyone of many things.

They looked around the room without saying anything else until the host returned. She served them their drinks. They took a moment to take a sip of them before striking up a conversation.

— So you get direct light through those large windows. It is a nice view that you have, he said.

— Oh, when I moved in it was a hidden view, but I wanted to be able to see the garden and I had those windows put in.

— Your house is handsomely furnished.

— Thank you. I'm rather somewhat of a collector of things as you see.

— Then I noticed that on that pedestal that there's a familiar figure, he said.

A bust of a life-size stone statue was in the sunlight.

— Well, the Socialist Realists wanted their leaders to be recognizable to their followers. I believe there's a story behind it. I don't know what it is.

They smiled knowingly.

— In truth, it was a present given to me by someone I knew who had suffered persecution during that troubled time, she said.

— Yes, we have to be thankful that those unfriendly regimes mostly disappeared. And it was intolerable to live in mortal fear and not know where the next meal was coming from, he said.

— But still it's terrible for others elsewhere for the same reasons, Mr. Elrod, said Karol.

— We're the fortunate ones, he said.

— It doesn't help others that we think that though.

— It's the way of the world. There's nothing we can do about it.

— You don't think there is.

— Not expediently.

— I'd like to think otherwise, but you're probably right.

— I wish I wasn't.

He had finished his drink. He said he had to be going. They walked with him to the door.

— And as we're on the subject I might mention that our elections are upcoming and I'm on the ballot again. And I can't pass up an opportunity to encourage members of the electorate to cast their votes.

Then consequently he offered to send information to them that they might like to have to help make an informed decision. He flattered them for what such a decision entailed. And for their votes that they might cast in his favour, he thanked them. He picked up the bag.

— I thank you again for your help, said Miss MacSweeney.

— I am glad to oblige.

Inside the two women sat back down.

The sunlight was perhaps even more reflectively and brightly shining off the polished surface of the stone statue.

— I had no idea who any of the municipal councillors were, said Miss MacSweeney.

— He's one of the active councillors who goes after people for votes. It's surprising he doesn't try to buy them. I don't know how he gets anyone to vote for him. But he always wins. Maybe it's because it's for the municipal elections that few care as we should. So then he didn't seem to appreciate your sculpture for what's interesting about it and not too obvious; and there appears to be more to it than meets the eye. That expression on his face gives the impression of a man having had a strong bearing.

— He's quizzical looking, I've always thought.

— I think there are associations to make that have been objectified. He looks ordinary, and his features are rounded and personable and the political, historical, and the personal side create tension. That's what has been subtly objectified. It is an original work, which wasn't the idea probably.

Then Karol said that as an architect that she had a vocational interest in the study of the social sciences, as in her line of work it was important that, "We understand what the reasons are for building the buildings we want to build and live in."

— It's incumbent of those in the profession to keep up on how styles are forever changing and are always about to.

She also affirmed how sometimes for that reason that she enjoyed reading historically set novels at her leisure.

The Unorthodox Ox

Mary-Adeline followed suit and related that as she was a musician, she was interested in considering influences that made for different musical trends.

They were agreeing to agree and disagree as to why past events might have occurred in some way or another.

Mary-Adeline offered to refresh her drink. She poured more ice tea for her.

— So you're a collector of conversation pieces that are of interest, you said.

Karol was pointing at a collection of small ornate bottles that were set out on a display table.

— I have a habit of acquiring curiosities that I come across, said Miss MacSweeney.

— Those are interesting. Are they antiques? For perfume, I should imagine.

— They're snuff bottles. They were for snuff.

— I'd have thought they were for perfume.

— Snuff was popular in China at one time. The Chinese were connoisseurs of snuff.

— Then it wouldn't be such an awful habit if one kept snuff in those exquisite bottles? They are intricately carved.

— It was illegal to smoke tobacco. It was a capital crime to smoke. But snorting snuff was legal. It was prescribed as a remedy for colds and stomach ailments, but later smoking became legal and snuff was not as popular.

— Yes, it's funny how there are certain activities that are acceptable and become unacceptable and fall out of favour or might come back. Then coincidentally, for what I'm going to be working on, I was reading up on punishments that people are capable of exacting upon each other, that the poor and women have suffered from the most. And what were past offenses are hard to imagine that they could be considered to be offenses, and they were severely punished. Gossiping was once a punishable crime. Then I just came across a drawing of a device, that had a rod with knives on it. It was put into an offender's mouth to curb the person's tongue, I guess was the idea. Imagine what the man was like who came up with that invention. Someone who had to have been afraid of what people were saying about him. But it's normal to gossip a little. How can we live without gossiping? Anyway, at least now we can gossip more freely than in the past. Though that's not always a good thing.

She picked up a bottle and uncorked it. She sniffed at the opening.

— The Chinese disguised their disgusting snuff in these beautiful little bottles. It doesn't smell of tobacco any more.

— That is from the 1650s.

— I'll be careful not to drop it.

She corked the bottle and set it down.

— Then my husband came to tell you what happened. So on his behalf, I'd like to ask you to pardon him if he was impolite. He can be brutish sometimes and he doesn't understand that he has crossed the line. And I remember the first impression I had when we met that I can't forget. Then now we're newlyweds, though in fact, we've been married for years really. And I shouldn't say so, but I think I've married the wrong man and I'm disappointed already. I've made a mistake I'm afraid. But I ought not to be talking like this and gossiping.

Then against the outside window a bird flew into the plate glass. The noise startled them. They stood up to look out the window. A songbird was on the ground lying motionless.

— I must hang up new ribbons outside. The storm yesterday blew them off.

— It was a wild storm.

— Yes, there was damage in my garden.

— But it has been a good season for the weather. Farmers aren't complaining as they do. You've had a good yield for what you grow, too?

— It has been a good summer, perfect really.

— So I wonder, I suspect you don't sell vegetables for the money. Your prices are such a bargain.

— I sell them because I have more than I know what to do with and if I didn't and gave them away, there might be a sense of obligation in return. I know I overcompensate for what I expect animals and insects to make off with. But to grow more is almost the same effort as to grow less.

The songbird was on its feet chirping, hopping, ready to fly off.

— Then it's fortunate perhaps that my cat isn't around. He'd

The Unorthodox Ox

have brought that bird into the house, said Mary-Adeline.

— Oh, cats are hard to tame. They're wild animals. And I suppose I might tell you that when he stopped by our house I fed him when he wouldn't stop begging. And one day he came in and he made a terrible mess. I admit to having had to kick him out the door. I have to say that I feel bad about it now and somewhat guilty.

— Sam was mischievous.

The bird flew off. Her phone was then ringing.

— I should be going.

— It's all right. I'll let it ring.

— I should go.

— I can listen to the message later.

The phone stopped ringing. But Karol was going to leave.

Then they hoped they would speak more often and get to know each other better.

— I'm so sorry for what happened.

— Thank you.

Then she asked when leaving what the vegetables that were ripening were soon going to be.

§

Earlier when outside she had missed several calls. One was from Harold to warn her of Karol's visit.

The other messages that she listened to, they were from friends of hers getting back to her to accept the invitation for her evening meal. The plans that she had had for the evening were to cook for invited friends.

Cooking was a pastime and a passion for her, and with an abundant fresh source of produce she knew what to do with what she grew. She was an aficionado of occidental and traditional cuisines that were similar in origin as to what were the influences that made up the repertoire of the music she performed, from the French, Italian, and Spanish traditions.

She was a devotee of diverse cross-cultural fusion cuisines and was doubtlessly motivated and interested in experimenting with what are often considered to be incompatible ingredients. So it was throughout and during preparations: dicing and slicing and what was an elaborate and complex cooking process, that there were specific characteristic flavours and different combinations at play, then how each of them respected the singular individuality of every flavour; they stood out, yet harmonized in a complementing manner, all with one another, as if it were a family reunion of tastes who when assembled together would whoop it up in the pleasure centres of the brain and thereafter they embedded themselves down into long-term memory.

The friends who attended her suppers were musicians, composers, singers, writers, scientists, museum curators, businessmen and women, and academics, who in praising the food before them would say more than what was asked of them and always asked for more.

She called her invited guests back to cancel the evening's supper, as the prospect then of an affair of the heart and the mind had given rise to emotional forces that ought not to be taken for granted. But that was not the subject to question and rather it was the subject who was the question and regarding him, in his defence; contrary to what his wife had said, he, as he had appeared to her, was the kind of individual who looked as if he was capable of knowing how to take the lid off of emotions that are kept in reserve, and such uncommon men are unusual to come across and one must enjoy their unearthly appearance and think their coming was in the stars. The evidence for such an evaluation for what was to remain optimistically a lasting impression was credible enough, considering how he had come to her, emerging from the storm with such terrible news to tell her. There had been the measured reaction to her invitation, the manner in which he accepted it, eagerly, but not over-anxiously. There had been a natural unease he had been comfortable with when he had come in through the front door dripping and shivering, looking unarmed. She had brushed by him when she closed the door after him. His natural scent and her fragrance had mingled. She had watched him dry himself off with a towel with his clothes still on. She had wanted to tell him to get out of his wet clothes, though had waited to make the suggestion, and so then the shy awkwardness of the procrastinating until the waiting was over. They had lit the fire together and blown on it to get it roaring. She had laid down on the floor by his feet and had asked him to sit down next to her in front of the warmth of the fire, which at first had appeared to have been an innocent and friendly invitation.

Then how he had looked at her, as if lost in the revelation of an awakening discovery, and she had seen that he realized that if he were to find out what that discovery was he'd have to act on his impulses as she had, and after more encouragement and when he acted upon those impulses, she had asked him who he was, but without waiting for his answer she decided for him. He was someone. A lone man who might have fallen from the sky.

Then she had heard the sound of his heart beating loudly and it had felt to her as if it had been her own.

That the previous night could repeat itself she had no reason to deny.

She would make plans for him to come and enjoy a meal, and they would gorge themselves.

§

If he were to have had no choice than to go on with what would have been a decidedly ongoing omen for the future, and for as long as he would have got away with it. But what then would happen when the truth would eventually come to light? How would he have accounted for the lies that he certainly would have lost track of? But then perhaps Mary-Adeline would have gone her way along the way. There should have been no reason for him to worry? However, he was to go over scenarios.

Then he ought to have maybe suspected or known without becoming distressed, that there was not much for him to accomplish by getting riled up and testing himself to the limit of his ability to do so, and he could have reconciled himself then to the obvious realization, no matter how discomfiting, that there was no escape from what would not have provided him with relief from the speculations that he was apprehensively entertaining.

But what if then, by happenstance, if he were to have been called upon to jump onto a passing horse that was galloping by and by an enigmatical biblical twist of fate if he were to ride out as one of the four horsemen of the apocalypse (the fourth?)? But in that unlikelihood he would not have known how to react to what he would have had to have known to be inconceivable when fighting for his peace of mind on a battlefield of madmen, and in what would have been a gesture for control, he would have at first, tentatively, pulled back on the reins of the horse that was running away beneath him, and he would have struggled to think about what were the consequences and possibilities and for what was going to be the rest of his life from the previous night onward.

He was blinking his eyes. His hands before him were resting on his office desk. He let out a deep long resonant sigh from a breath he had inhaled deeply.

But he was not going to be saved from making a decision that he would have to make one way or another.

Then his day's work was about to begin, and the same as on every work day it was to go on past the time when he should have gone home and left his work troubles behind. His work day was beginning, and he was not going to be saved from it either, from working himself into the usual state of aggravation as the long day in his office would drag on and on.

So it was in their conversation, when he was talking to her about those who in their work are disappointed by what they do, that he had referred to a study that he had known about that had investigated what provides job satisfaction for working men and women, especially for the fortunate few who happen to be lucky enough (if only for a brief time) to be in the pursuit of an ideal when working. Then the results of the cited study and of others had suggested maybe that working for a cause was not important, and that determination is probably correct and would have to do with so many not being able to admit to being slaves to necessity and that or a similar conclusion might convince a working man or woman that they are wanted and appreciated, despite evidence to the contrary, and so this could explain the tendency that hard-working workers have for praising labours that are neither for love nor profit and is an excuse for why it is comforting to remember on-the-job memories and why labourers like to talk about their earlier days in poverty and remember acquaintances who are dead and who may have died on the job. It is why those who are destitute can boast of having been exploited. And it is a little of such considerations that can and will inspire a class of men and women to trod on into old age, no further ahead at the end than in the beginning from their first day in the shop or on the office floor.

That was what they had been discussing, before it had been no longer necessary to say another word as they were whispering romantic instructions on how to proceed.

Then he had been happy once with what he did, early on when he was in the fields observing birds, plants, insects, and noting the changes in the seasons and that had been a time and a place to be surrounded by living things that seized the man by his nose, ears, and eyes. It had been what he had said was like being "cradled in the arms of mother nature", when out collecting samples and foraging in the fields, forests, and swamps. So he was pleased to have thought himself to be a part of it all.

But from those days and from that time he had spent, what were the carefree hours, when out romping in the wild, he had moved on to complete an education, and he had acquired scientific expertise and he had gone on into undertaking specialized research and he had mastered skills that are necessary to have a grasp of, so as to know how to set up statistical models; then he also had created methods for putting them to use.

And during those years, to administrators who had witnessed professionally his progress, he had shown himself to have had administrative skills — that he was good at picking up on definable priorities — that he knew how to coordinate diverse operative ideas. Such abilities had recommended him and he had risen up through the ranks from one job to the next, one department to the next one above until he had settled down into the position he had been in for some time where he politically managed variable interests that worked for him, and so he was responsible for coordinating the work of his people in his department and for those connected to his department and for those in some other connected departments and for close or distant colleagues or associates who looked to him for guidance, encouragement and sympathy, and to complain, rant, rage, accuse, threaten and blame. More often than not the latter set of encounters were the most frequent.

But then the success of his own ambitiousness had been worrisome. Of course, he had known what the drawbacks were in exercising authority. He had not been naïve as to what the sacrifices were that had to be made, and for what is won, compared to what is in exchange lost. But to possess sought after skills and not to have given into the temptation to rise above those beneath him would have been difficult to pass up.

Then how regrettable and inevitable it was that there were so many within the immediate proximity who were bitter from the same dissatisfactions that anyone is sour from, and they made his and their own working lives a living hell.

He led the devising and the planning of studies. He was in charge of monitoring them as they progressed. His time he spent in his office, if not in meetings, reading, writing, and rewriting reports. He answered memos, messages, and calls. He dealt with conflicting differences of opinion and looked after measuring the unpredictability of the outcome of the decisions that he would have to aptly make.

Then at that moment, on his desk, there was a report to open and for him to read: the *Japanese Rhino Beetle Report*. He opened it and he read "The Abstract" that anticipated instrumentally the ideas for the text in the pages to follow, as to what they were factually to be about, and he read to the end of the Abstract of the *Rhino Beetle Report* and would have successively read the complete report and have concentrated his efforts on what he would have had to analyse, and so put aside thinking about anything to do with a decision that he might have made concerning his romantic adventure.

But what happened then was an interruption of the routine kind, and it could have been any one of so many interruptions. In his office doorway was standing a woman. He saw why she was there. He invited her to come in. The woman was unsure yet she crossed what was the unfamiliar space. He further welcomed her, and he commented on what was the evident reason for the interruption.

— It looks like it's a Pickerel and not a Northern Leopard. I can't tell which. I'm not convinced either way, which is what it means when we don't know what to think. Who would disagree if we don't know what to think? he asked her.

The woman was holding in her hand a stuffed frog that was not identifiable as either a Pickerel or a Northern Leopard. That explained his confusion. She offered for him to take the stuffed frog. He saved himself the trouble of taking it from her and having to give it back. But he had a closer look at it, inclining himself forward in his chair. She gave it a squeeze. It let out the sound of a small electronic croak that might have mildly amused someone other than himself. She understood that she would not squeeze it a second time.

The stuffed frog was scaled to be a quarter larger in size than what would have been an average adult specimen. It had human features. Over half closed eyes eyelashes curled upward. The tip of a red velvet tongue was hanging from its open mouth. A nylon material for the skin was shiny.

— You're Gwendolyn Llewellyn from the Darwin Foundation, a survivor? he asked.

— I am.

— But someday none of us will survive. I hope I am not right. I might be. You were to show that frog to me?

— I was asked to introduce myself, and I've a message to pass on, she gave him the message.

— Would anyone have told you why? Or perhaps you've made an educated guess or an uneducated one. It would have to be an educated one.

She confirmed that she had been targeted for not being as informed as she might have been.

— Then the cruel joke at your expense was to have to bring a stuffed frog to me.

She smiled for being the victim.

The head of a lamp on his desk he aimed to shed more light on the specimen.

— It has sleepy eyes to suggest the long winter of their hibernation. Or the eyes are like that because it was cheaper than to have sewn on eyes. So then no one has told you what you will need to know, which is the standard practice in most work environments.

— I have been given written materials to read.

— That's a start to begin with.

He leaned back in his chair into an accommodating position, clasped his hands behind his head, stretched his elbows backwards, pointed one elbow upwards. She made her own adjustments.

— I might save you the trouble of having to figure out what is or isn't obvious or relevant and for what we ought to know but what we don't. A background because the foreground isn't staring us in the face. A summing up, it's no trouble. I hope not. I prefer not to go to the trouble if it is too much trouble. Think of this as being necessary or unnecessary if it is not.

He then provided the new intern with an overview of *The Frogwatch Program*. He went over the guidelines for what they were. He explained how volunteers had been going out into wetland areas and following the guidelines and that tens of thousands of volunteers from the general public were recording variations in the changing sound-scape of frog croakings.

He outlined the organizational workings, he spoke about those involved. He explained how the data was being analyzed that they were interpreting, what the conclusions would mean, and what was going to happen. What the research would accomplish, he underscored. He concluded then in the final point that he made, that a last call would go out and environmentalists, botanists, biologists, field naturalists, pollution experts, park rangers, government officials, and a passel of committed individuals would make a petition for humankind to step back from the brink.

— There will be survivors, he laughed.

He evaluated administrative concerns, accounting for difficulties that come up when interests are working at cross-purposes. On that subject he spoke about how success can be compromised with the introduction of new procedures in the middle of a process that is better to do early on when considering other facets in order to guarantee how things will work smoothly throughout, rather than improvising on the fly and throwing a wrench into the works in the middle of it. And he said to the intern that many were wrong in their thinking that the world's problems were not of their making and of others.

— It's an unhealthy view to subscribe to. It does not help anyone to believe that, he said.

But he agreed in part with the idea, that is to say to hope for the best, like so many, but he was then the one, in his position, who would always have to take on more than someone's fair share of the overall responsibility and everyone else's, as for what was being inexpertly executed and poorly realized, which is when he, as one of the more seemingly responsible individuals, would have to attend to problems after it was too late and that is when a man responsible is burdened beyond the point of what a person is able to reasonably withstand.

The Unorthodox Ox

He took the stuffed frog from her. He set it down on his desk under the lamplight.

— That's as helpful as I can probably be for the time being, Ms. Llewellyn.

She was grateful for his counsel she said.

— Ask questions of others. It never hurts to get other opinions. You will do well then.

She said she would.

He walked her to the door. He sat back down at his desk. He was looking at the time that had passed, and he looked at the stuffed frog and he was considering maybe what the mistake about it was suggesting. But that it was a Pickerel or a Northern Leopard or neither one nor the other, that was not the crux of it, no.

He was looking at the *Japanese Rhino Beetle Report* that he was going to avoid for the moment.

Then the message for him to make a call he read, and he got up to pace around in his office. So he was mulling over again what he had been thinking about before.

Then the call that the message was asking him to make he made.

— I hope I'm not disturbing you too much, if you happen to be busy? Karol straight away asked him.

— I am not, that's why I'm calling, Karol.

— Tell me if you are busy, Harold.

— I'm calling as I've a moment and I got your message.

— Well, I wanted to tell you about my visit with Mary-Adeline MacSweeney, but if you're occupied.

— I have a moment.

— Then I visited with her. She was troubled about what had happened. And when I arrived Councillor Elrod was there. He had brought along her cat's remains to give them to her. He thought that she wanted to have the remains. Imagine.

— Did he?

— But I think he was there to solicit her vote. She invited us in for a refreshment. I had no idea she was such a well-known musician. Then she's knowledgeable about things, which is natural for someone as accomplished as she has to be. It would be surprising if she was ill-informed. She served us ice tea and tea biscuits.

— She appreciated your concern then?

— I didn't ask, I think so. But I did ask her what she will have for us next week, aubergines. She would have planted them early. She was a little standoffish.

— If she's upset that would be understandable.

— Then when on my way home I happened to run into Trudi Brown, and she told me that when she was riding her bicycle by our house last night that she had seen you almost naked outside in your underwear. I think she thought I had kicked you out of the house for some reason. At first she thought you were stark naked. That would have been exciting for her.

— I was in my underwear.

— That poor woman is having problems. But she let on that I had a problem if my husband is running around outside in the middle of the night in his underwear. I thought it was that buffoon of a neighbour she was referring to.

— It was me.

— I hope I don't have to ask you why?

— You can if you like.

— I don't think I will. Anyway, I'm going to come into town this afternoon and I'll stop by, and I would like to tell you something that I shouldn't keep from you. It's about a contract offer I've had. It can wait until I tell you. I'll come by after lunch. Are you going out for lunch maybe?

— I'm about to.

— I wish I could join you. We haven't gone out for lunch in ages.

— It will have to be another time. I'm about to go out now.

— Where are you going?

— I've yet to decide.

— You will have to decide if you're about to go out? Won't you?

— I will.

— Don't ask me to tell you where you should go.

— I wouldn't have thought of asking.

— You were. Don't deny it. You were going to.

— Now I won't.

— All right, be that way, if you want. Then I wouldn't tell you where to go even if you were to ask.

— I'd appreciate it if you wouldn't.

— I won't.

The Unorthodox Ox

— Good.

He might have made up his mind to satisfy her.

— Have a good lunch.

— Likewise.

— Then don't over-indulge and make an absolute pig yourself, if you can help it, Harold.

— I shall try not to.

— Try not to embarrass me in my absence, if you can help it.

— I won't.

She would see him later that afternoon she promised.

Then it was the lunch hour and he headed out with others going down in an elevator. He went out of the building into the streets. He had to refuse to eat in the company of work colleagues, as that would have complicated his choice as to where he might have wanted to go, and he was still deciding where.

So he set off towards an area of restaurants, and he actually was not to second-guess himself as to where he was going: *Chez Henri Lai*, what was an establishment, where impressions for what they were, as they intended to be, were not left to chance, and from the outside, what was the outward front exterior, and when going inside and upon immediate entry, the effect, as intended, was to arouse the appetites of diners who were being seated at their tables. Then it was artful and also moreover significant that on the walls was a series of paintings hanging, panels, that depicted pastoral scenes, where men and women were feasting in the company of domestic and wild animals, with donkeys, horses, stags and does. The animals were indulging themselves in lush gardens. The smiling ruminants had in their mouths fresh grass and in life if they were to have eaten too much of it, that likely would have fatally bloated them. The table place settings were of refinement, of note were hand-woven linen tablecloths on which laid out was designed handcrafted English sterling silver cutlery and by making use of it, that would have made a meal more enjoyable, due to the value of those prized utensils.

He was welcomed as a familiar customer and seated at a table beneath a painting of a portrait of a half-naked man-goat.

From the table d'hôte, for the first course, he selected the oxtail soup that was rewarding in sustenance as was the main course that offered surprises of a pleasant sort. He ate for his pleasure and to his fill a satisfactory amount. For dessert he had a mousse au chocolat aux noisettes au whiskey in order to over-indulge and make somewhat a pig of himself. It was rich and not easily digested, it produced a mild unsettling effect. Then he paid the bill before he had finished eating the last morsel of his mousse or having a digestif or coffee, and he went out to relieve his digestive discomfort in the fresh air.

He was going along for a while with a passing crowd, walking his meal off and it was after several blocks that he entered into a part of the city that was outside of the central business section. Fewer people were about. He was further off-track than advisable.

Then it was from on the other side of the street from where he was walking. A woman called out to him. He looked but did not answer her question nor her request.

White clouds were coming into the sky for effect.

He came to a district of warehouses where for a moment he stopped at a loading zone to join in with a group of men, who were watching the unloading off trucks of unmarked boxes, unexceptional crates, and nondescript packages. So there was an ambivalent air about the loitering men, which might have occasioned them to move on to find work or if lucky get to work. He was one of the lucky ones. He set off to go back to his office.

But it was from up the street then and along where he was going, coming down was a line of cars. A wedding procession, it drove by. Revellers from out open car windows were calling out. Horns were honking.

A bank of darker clouds blew over. Other far away horns blew in the distance.

Such an occurrence would not only have to do with what was occurring in the description of that moment.

Then it was from down the other end of the street that there was a line of black cars, a funeral procession, turning from around a corner. It was coming slowly down the street. The cars pulled up to the front of a funeral home. Mourners got out of the vehicles. They gathered together on the sidewalk. Pedestrians made way for them. Out of the funeral home the director came out. He welcomed his clients to come inside. The pedestrians were moving on. Light rain began falling.

He was standing and watching those proceedings when the last car of the procession pulled up before him. A man got out of his car, who addressed him and said.

— You saw that couple who would have got married for love or maybe for even money? I'd place my bets on the money being the safest bet. And were you maybe one of her last lovers, one of the last ones? Then you don't look like it. I'm sorry if you were. I have to accuse someone. Then a few of them will be here today mourning her passing. No, I see you couldn't be one of those she told me about. And I see you're not here for the visitation.

The man was distraught and had to have been crying for some time.

— You're not for the visitation. Oh, I am sorry. Ah, this is complicated. It's confusing. I'm trying to cope as best I can. I'm not coping well. Then I know that I'm about to say something that I will regret for who knows how long? I am about to say something like that, and I'm sorry about it already. So let me make it up to you, sir. Would you maybe like to come in for the visitation? You'd be welcome. I'd certainly be pleased to have the company. I wouldn't mind having someone to talk to right now. I don't think I should be alone at a time like this. I know I shouldn't be. But I didn't know who to invite to come with me to comfort me. I couldn't think of anyone who could come with me and see me through this difficult time. It could as well be a stranger, don't you think?

Harold said he could.

— That's kind of you. And I wouldn't agree. I'd think I was a lunatic and I am. But we are all insane.

— We are.

— I know I shouldn't trouble others.

— It's all right. I understand.

The funeral director ushered them inside.

— I know that I am not going to be able to stop myself from thinking about what bothers me so much about what has happened. I just can't see how I will be able to get over this. Then the casket should be open. It should be. I don't know if it is to be open. It ought to be as she was beautiful. And it's not a good idea to have an open casket if it's for an ugly cur. It will be closed for me. Unless that will be the final indignity that I will have to endure. I hope not for the sake of those who will be present.

They entered the visitation room. The woman in the casket was young.

— Is she not beautiful? he asked sadly.

Harold nodded and said she was.

— You are someone who appreciates beauty?

— I am.

— There is so much in the world that's beautiful. There is. Isn't there? It can take your breath away. Then beauty for someone like me is like a promise that there has to be something better out there. So we're surrounded by so much beauty, for those of us who are as ugly as sin. I bet you don't know what it is like to look in the mirror each morning and recoil at the sight of one's self. You can't conceive of what it's like.

— Oh, I can.

— It is not how we see things either.

— It isn't.

— I was in love with her, but I was only a friend. Then she used to talk to me about her love affairs. What I know about her intimate personal life. And someone who is responsible for what happened to her is here today, but I can't figure out who he would be. She didn't tell me everything. She didn't tell me everything. But how can we tell anyone everything?

The man gave him his name, Raunce, and he continued to pour his heart out about his monstrosities and lowly attributes, and further he confessed to suffering from unrequited love.

The young deceased woman had not known any better. She had been interested in bad men.

More was said. Harold had to go.

— You're someone who admires beauty. I appreciate that. Then it is good to know there are those of us who are giving the philistines a run for their money.

The man Raunce invited him to attend the funeral for the following day, and he had not had the heart to turn down the invitation, but he would not have gone.

The sky was clouding up, but it had stopped raining.

So for him to have happened onto the visitation, as unanticipated as it was, had given rise to ideas and thoughts that were in keeping with the problems that he was wrestling with.

The Unorthodox Ox

Then it was when she asked him, that is to say, when Mary-Adeline was pointedly asking him, "Tell me a little about yourself?" He had told her how he thought that there were consequences in giving the impression of being too curious. "Impossible things happen to me sometimes. I almost can't believe them." He had said. She had said, "I too am curious as well."

So how unlikely it was that she had honoured him and he was honoured, as the promise of love, no matter how deserving, is a great honour. "You're sad?" She had asked him.

At times he had been complimented for his melancholy. But to be a sad man is not enough to bring on feelings of reciprocity. It can have the opposite effect, engender pity and scorn, but it had been a compliment. But why worry? When he could consider how she had been generous with her feelings and with her attentions, her memories. She had attended to his burn, it had almost begun to heal miraculously (it was a miracle). Then she had told him how as a child that she had been a prodigy, and how luckily she had managed to live up to that enormous promise.

He couldn't maybe make heads or tails of it, why and how, who or what he was: a morphologist, a physiologist, a field naturalist, a paleoclimatologist, a cosmographer, an entomologist, an inveterate biophiliac, an administrator, a man of the people, whoever they were. Who was he? And that had been kindly put to him by the flames of a dying fire.

"Me?" he asked himself as he looked into a glass window that he passed, behind which was an empty display case.

He was returning to work.

He took the elevator up to the top floor of the office building. He looked for but did not find the hidden key that opened the rooftop door that led out onto the roof. But that was not important as he did not have a need to go out on to the roof, and cutting short what would have been to avoid the work he had yet to complete, he went down to his office.

He got back to working through the *Japanese Rhino Beetle Report,* and he was to analyse conclusions that led to other conclusions and indicated how the probable cause for the Rhino Beetle's difficulties was uncertain, so there were secondary matters in need of further investigation, although it was evident that the decreasing number of Rhinos had to do with reproduction and their inability to replace their declining numbers was worsening, and it was as he was working on what would have been the different reasons that he was comparing the mating habits of various insects, as to how different species make use of their sharp claws, oversized jaws, and sticky fingers to grab ahold of their mating partners and hang on for dear life. Therein was the dilemma "how"?

But for a research entomologist to morosely conjecture that there is a valid comparison to make between man and insect, that should be inconceivable, if when understanding how terrible the war has been that has gone on between man and bug and if recognizing what have been the horrors that victims have endured through the ages. But nevertheless, despite the suffering and the unaccounted for ramifications that millions have suffered from at the hands of insects, or perhaps because of it, it is possible to appreciate that the sometimes vilified field of entomology is an informative science to look into and interesting to know more about and it offers an understanding about life and death and it is interesting for those interested in wanting to know more about what there is to know about the domain of the insect kingdom; it is a fascinating subject that an expert in the field can never claim to fully master.

His specialization that he was so keenly and personally interested in had been for the beetle, that is the largest family of insects, accounting for twenty percent of the earth's biomass; so it is that investigatively: the coleoptera is studied and researched for its design, the elytras, for the wide industrious range of its determined activities, and the beetle, similar to other insects is obviously accredited for having superhuman and exceptional proportional strength comparably and they are noted for having a hard outer shell that protects the little beetle's vulnerable underbellies, and there are those features that beetles possess that if present in other life forms would increase the survival of some and make for a better way of life for others.

The notes for those who were to do the final revisions on the *Japanese Rhino Beetle Report* he finished.

Then while engaged and seriously still contemplating other entomological imponderables, into his office came his assistant. She announced her presence, and she was to tell him that his wife had arrived. She asked him if she should show Karol in. He asked whether there was anything scheduled for him to take care of, for what was on his agenda to look after, but he answered his own question and he asked others.

— You should tell her to wait? But what would happen if I left her sitting out there to fester for a while? Did she look like she could fester away for any length of time? Was she in a festering mode?

His assistant might have thought to have advised him, but knew what not to say.

— So the *Rhino Report* then is all right. Though the results are not too conclusive, nothing ever is. And I'm thinking about next week. What about next week then?

He asked her about the following week, how the days were shaping up. Were there problems she could warn him about? She informed him that the latest reports would be ready for him. That was helpful to know. There was nothing out of the ordinary. That was good to know as well. He instructed her to pass the *Japanese Rhino Beetle Report* along to those concerned.

— I'll let her wait for a while. And everything is all right or I only think so.

She took away the report.

He was looking out his office window at a cloud that was passing by, for how long he lost track. It had been raining again and for how long he did not know either. Neither then did he know how long Karol would be waiting before he would send for her, and so it was to be a matter of him being reminded to send for her.

Her coming to see him in his office was rare. He had not not forgotten her other unwarranted and previous interruptions. His assistant eventually called him to tell him that his wife was still waiting and she was maybe beginning to fester in the waiting room, as he had suspected might happen.

Karol came charging into his office.

— Behind in your work, as usual, are you, Harold? she asked.
— Not more so than usual really.
— You have to be more efficient.
— No, efficiency can be overrated.
— You'd think that, of course.

She was standing in front of his desk across from him.

— May I?
She sat down without waiting for his permission.
— Take a seat, if you'd like.
— But what a mess in here. Am I to come down and clean up after you in your office? Is that why I'm here?
From his desk she picked up a pile of papers. She evened out the edges along the vertical and the horizontal sides. She thumped the pile down before him to emphasize her complaint.
— How do you get anything done with it like this? I can see why you don't.
— How can I answer that?
— As best you can.
— I have already.
— Then you received your amphibians?
She picked up the stuffed frog from under the lamp, she tossed it up and grabbed it out of the air. It let out a croak.
— It makes a noise. How cute. Am I being too nosy?
— I wouldn't be one to say you are.
— Who would be?
— Anyone but me, I think.
She picked up a copy of the *Frogwatch Observation Form* that was on top of the papers she had straightened up.
— This has to be your form for it. It says it is. It is. Isn't it?
He was looking out the window at a low passing cloud.
— It doesn't look too complicated. You would have to hope it wouldn't be, she said.
He hoped so as well.
— The form suggests that commitment is required and necessary.
— Yes, it does say that.
— You want the time of day. When would that be? In the evenings or in the mornings maybe, I would have to guess.
— If convenient.
— For those committed. Then what if we participated? You and I. We could. You could take me out on a date into a marsh? That would be something to do.
— I wouldn't think so.
— Why not? I think so. Why couldn't we? I think we can participate in your program if we wanted to.

— There is no need for us to do so. I don't think we'd want to.

— I think we could. I'll fill out your form. I'll tell you if it is complicated. Then you've said yourself the simplest things are sometimes the most complicated or vice versa.

— The reverse is true that is correct.

— We can do our part. I'd like us to participate. Then I'll get to know more about what you're doing. So starting this evening? Yes, we'll go out this evening. You can take me out on a date into a dank swamp. I should think you'd be begging me to and have always wanted to.

She tossed the frog to him. He caught it and put it back under the lamp. She folded up the *Frogwatch Observation Form* to take away for her keeping.

— Then you do not want me to torment you, and you don't need my help for that, I know, she said.

— I don't.

— Then do you have to keep working?

— Not if I won't get anything else done.

— I am rescuing you. And we should be on our honeymoon now. But you're too busy and unable to get anything done on time. If you were more efficient, Harold. Can you leave now?

— If you give me no choice.

— I give you no choice.

— Yes, we can leave.

They went out through the maze of office cubicles, along the corridors. They went down in the elevator into the basement garage. Then as they were going she was telling him what she had to tell him. He listened to her and he did not ask her questions that needed explanation.

— I don't have to tell you not to mention this to anyone. Not a word to anyone yet.

— I won't.

— I'm telling you, you won't. So I wish we could have gone away on our honeymoon. Now neither of us has the time.

— I thought you said it wasn't too important.

— I was only saying so, wasn't I?

Then as they got to their cars, she told him that she had gone out that afternoon and she had thought to buy a copy of a recording of Miss MacSweeney's, as she had been interested to see what the musician's fame was about, she said. And it occurred to her that he might like to listen to the recording while he was driving home. She thought he would enjoy it. She got from her car the disc to give to him.

— Drive carefully, the roads are slippery, she said.

— I shall heed your advisory.

Over the car radio an announcer was forecasting continuing variable weather. Unpredictable showers were to persist. Then an attendant in a parking booth to whom he paid for the day's parking was listening to the same forecast. The attendant commented when giving him back his change that it was not going to snow out of season at least.

At a stoplight and waiting for the light, he took up the recording. On the cover of its liner was a picture of Mary-Adeline MacSweeney. She was on a stage in a concert hall in front of an orchestra. An audience was on its feet before her. The audience was applauding. A young child was presenting a bouquet of flowers to her. The maestro had his arm on her shoulder.

So there would have followed a night of celebration, and afterwards and at a later date there was the mixing session in a recording studio with a sound engineer to remix that night's performance. What memories she had to have had: the concert, the applause, the studio time, and the royalties that were to come rolling in over the years.

Then he was to listen to what he was to come to know as being a musical version of what he would have believed to be the truth about music itself and almost about everything. A car behind him honked. He moved through the intersection.

He drove along throughout the movements of the concerto, through the fast and slow sections, out of the city into the countryside and along paved and onto gravel roads that passed through towns and open country fields.

Then when he arrived at the final chords, after Mary-Adeline had played a fiery cadenza that had reminded him of the previous night by the fire, he drove into their driveway. The music ended. He sat back in his seat, he closed his eyes and he attempted to relieve himself of his outrageous expectations. Karol drove up next to him.

The Unorthodox Ox

She got out of her car then into his.

— You can drive, she said.

— Off a cliff if you like, he grumbled.

They settled on where they were going.

— So I can't help but notice that you have not cleaned your car out in a while. I'm telling you to make sure you are aware of the fact. You appear not to be.

— I've been meaning to clean it.

He drove with his eyes on the road.

— You listened to it and you liked it, as you aren't complaining.

— I listened to it.

— I thought it was emotional. What's the word? Stirring? It was stirring. I'll be glad to tell her how much I liked it when I see her.

— It was stirring, that is the word, he said to her not wanting to add to her assessment.

— You had a bad day, I can tell.

— I'll clean the car out later.

He was driving over the speed limit on what was a winding stretch of road, careening around the curves, testing perhaps the manoeuvrability of the vehicle.

— So Karol, I was wondering what the damage was from the accident you had? I didn't notice anything.

— It was nothing. I hit a bump in the road and there was a thud and a rattle is all.

— There was a rattle. What rattle?

— I don't know.

— Where was the rattle?

— I couldn't tell you where the rattle was. How would I know?

— At the back, the front, at either side, under the frame?

She got out from her handbag the *Frogwatch Observation Form* to read it over.

— Where was the bump?

— Are you not driving too fast?

— Then you wouldn't be at all surprised if I hit a bump and there was a rattle, and if we went off the road and flying over a cliff?

— Slow down, would you?

He slowed down.

— On your form it asks that we give the date and the time. That makes a difference? Why does that make a difference?

— Those are variables.

— You have to say why. Your form isn't clear. I was right. I'm to write down the latitude and longitude? It asks.

— Minus 73 and 45.

— If it's a legal land description, Section, Township, Lot, or Concession. If there is a strong effluvium in the air. What would a strong effluvium mean?

— That there might be sewage or pollutants in the water, unless it's a bog with natural sources of methane.

— I can tell you're going to be grumpy as ever. I wish you wouldn't be.

— I'm tired. I had a lot on my mind today.

— I suppose I should have let you sleep last night and I didn't want to wake you up, but I was thinking we would have forgiven each other for everything.

— Have we?

— I wouldn't be too sure about that.

— Your apology I accept. He smiled.

— And I, yours?

— I hope so.

— I wouldn't be so sure if I were you as I might have a condition for you to meet. Are you interested in what it is?

— No.

— I haven't forgiven you then.

— I'd have suspected as much.

— Or maybe I will forgive you to be gracious. And Mother is always telling me what a fine man you are.

— You ought to be jealous of her for such a comment.

— She is jealous of me I think for everything.

— She has no reason to be.

— I'd like to think that, too.

He came to an access road and he drove by along stalks in the corn fields to the end of the road. They got out of the car. They walked out onto wet and soft ground to where there was open shallow water.

The sun was down on the horizon. A light breeze was blowing. Cattail seeds were floating through the reeds in the swamp.

The Unorthodox Ox

There were frogs and the odd toad croaking. She made her observations.

— So according to your form, the choice must be, it is.

She read from the *Frogwatch Observation Form*.

— *Calls are not overlapping, individuals can be counted, croakings are distinguishable.* I have to check the abundance code box "two"?

She checked the abundance code box number "two" with a pen.

— If the calls are distinguishable that tells us what? she asked.

— They are stressed.

— How are they stressed?

— Threatened.

— I'd like to know how, Harold.

— There is no way of knowing that.

— Look, if you don't want to be talkative at least you can say so. What's the problem?

— There isn't one.

— I don't believe you.

— That's the problem then.

— You want to be impossible. And you know I can be impossible.

— I do know that.

They listened to the frogs.

— Are the mosquitoes bothering you? she asked.

It was late in the season. There were no mosquitoes.

— Are we done here? Then we can go to another swamp? Would you like to?

He nodded.

— We can go to another one and to another, until you cheer up. God, I'm tired of you being uncooperative when you don't want to be. It can be tedious.

— Yet I'd like you to believe I don't mean to be.

— How am I supposed to believe that? Do you think?

— I'm afraid you aren't.

They went to another swamp further away on the outside of the farming areas, and there was an abundant number of frogs croaking in a loud and trumpeting chorus. She read out the corresponding choice.

— Abundance code box four: *full chorus, calls continuous and overlapping, individuals not distinguishable.* They are not stressed then?

— Less so. They're less stressed.

She checked the abundance code box "four".

— But I don't get it, there's no appreciable difference in the latitude and the longitude. It is the same here as where we were. We'd have to drive for hours or days to have the latitude and the longitude change and we've recorded the latitude and the longitude for two different locations, but it's the same, and they aren't far from each other and in one location the croaking is louder and in the other less so and the latitude and longitude didn't change. So the combined choices for the two marshes fall between the two and four abundance code boxes. Then what do you do? You take an average?

— We apply a function for random variables that are normally distributed.

— That's it?

— That's what we do.

The wind was dying. The frogs were croaking more quietly. Their calls were not continuous and not overlapping. Individuals were distinguishable. The cattail seeds were falling. The sun was disappearing. The moon was rising.

They stood still. He was quiet. She was the one to speak up after the volume level of the frog croaking was to resume as before.

— I wonder if you are having me on. Is that what you're trying to do now?

— I'm answering your questions, Karol.

— You could have fooled me. Looked like you weren't being serious.

— I was not fooling you.

— You could have been fooling me, I wouldn't have known one way or another.

— I don't either.

— Neither of us knows one way or another, who is fooling whom. Are you trying to get back at me for something now?

— How could I ever do that?

— That is a good question. You couldn't.

A bullfrog croaked a short distance from them.

The Unorthodox Ox

— Is it too late to drive anywhere else? she asked.
— It will be getting dark soon.
— If I didn't ask you anything you wouldn't say a thing.
— It is best not to ask then probably.

She ignored his unresponsiveness as they were going back, and maybe he seemed to be listening to what she was telling him.

She was relating to him a prediction; what the crops would be that were ripening in the fields, what the expected yield would be per acre, what the crop quality would be for what was to be soon harvested, if the rain let up. She spoke about the long-term weather, what it would be for the autumn, winter, the following spring, and what the five and ten year forecast might be according to the latest almanac.

— You'll tell me there's no credibility at all to an almanac. There isn't, but it's amusing. Then did you know, there's a section on animal husbandry? That's right. Animal husbandry, which is applicable in your case. So there's an entry for advice as to when to castrate farm animals. The best time to castrate. You might want to know when. The end of the month is the best time, in the last week, about now. And there's advice for sheering sheep. The best time for sheering sheep is the morning when the sun is coming up. The wool comes back thicker is why, is the explanation. There's a reason for sheering sheep at that time. I thought that was informative. But maybe you might tell me if you know of when there'd be another time that'd be good to castrate?

— I couldn't. No.

— You might tell me when would be the best time to get out the knife, she laughed. This is wonderful! I'm asking you the sort of annoying question that you like to needle me with to get on my nerves.

He thought for a moment to come up with a response.

— All right, I shall try to answer your question, as I have been trying to answer your questions.

He deliberated for a moment longer.

— Maybe when one animal has mounted another one. That would be the time to destesticulate them.

She laughed at his joke, and she was going to follow up with another question. He interrupted.

— For sheering sheep that would be better done after the mounting, he said.

— It's only superstition? But don't forget it is based on empirical evidence.

— And there's no denying experience.

— So you're giving me an opinion. You even made me laugh.

— If you're going to talk to me about castration I think it is necessary to defend myself. I have limits.

They knew how to discuss matters to determine maybe who was either right or wrong until there was little to say after arriving at a predictable stalemate.

— But Harold, if we're going to participate in this, what I want, is to enjoy ourselves. And don't think we're not going to, because I'm not going to let you off the hook. I know you don't want to, but it's only a few weeks before winter sets in and we need to get out before we're housebound. But I'm not interested in having a grumpy sourpuss at my side keeping me ill-company. I want you to be a good sport. I'd like you to make me laugh, and you're not making me laugh as you used to do. I remember when you made me laugh all the time. I remember that.

— I didn't mean to.

— I want you to amuse me more. I want you to be agreeable. Then tomorrow morning we'll come out here, and you can amuse me to no end. I hope you will.

— Not tomorrow, I can't. I'm supposed to attend a funeral tomorrow. I'm going to a funeral in the morning. A colleague's daughter died. He's not someone close. I wouldn't have mentioned him to you. It would look bad if I didn't attend.

He was surprised himself how the lie was so easy to come by.

— You're going to a funeral? she asked.

— I have no choice, I'm afraid.

— Oh? You don't?

— I'm going to have to get myself in the mood for it and assume a sad demeanour. She was a young woman.

— What are you saying? I'm not going to talk you out of it, am I?

— I imagine you wouldn't. She was young, and she had her whole life ahead of her apparently.

— You might have mentioned this.

The Unorthodox Ox

— I was going to and I just did.

She chose not to ask him anything about it.

Then before long she was again talking about what she wanted to say more about regarding what they earlier had spoken about in confidence. He listened as before.

He was driving at a speed she might have been comfortable with, but he should have slowed down more regardless.

Then when they were going past Mary-Adeline's house, he put the recording on. It blasted out as loud as it had been when he had been listening to it before. He turned down the volume. She adjusted it further to her liking.

— Are you trying to drown me out?

He did not answer her question.

— She has to be an exceptional individual, a genius, do you think? she asked.

— Yes undoubtedly.

— But we all have our talents.

— No, I think few have talent who have any idea of what to do with it.

— Yes, you would say that to be critical. And can you not be less critical? Then do you want to know what condition I have for you? I want you to be less critical. Also I would like you to clean out your car, if you would.

They were arriving home. She also was to say that there was yard work for him to do as well.

— That's a talent you've got. You're the handy man, Harold.

He remained outside. She went inside.

But he did not clean his car out or mow the lawn, prune any flowers or weed a flowerbed, and he headed off walking down the street. He was going along with a light heart and light on his feet.

The evening temperature was quickly dropping. The night was going to be fresh and cool.

§

It was in the yard of a neighbouring house, he was walking by, a small girl was playing with a fireplace log. She was holding the cut log up on its end and instructing it to not fall over. He said hello to the girl. She might have whispered back at him. He must have thought he heard something.

It was a new family that had moved in recently, she was still somewhat shy maybe, but she gave imperative instructions to the log that had tipped over and she threatened to burn it.

The girl's mother was coming out of the house to call her daughter in for supper, and the girl said to her mother that she was not going to go inside. She was not shy in refusing to do so. The mother came all the way out into the yard. The girl explained, "I won't come in. I am busy. Can you not see that? Are you blind as well as deaf?" The mother pleaded. The daughter answered, "Can you not go off and die and let me finish what I'm doing for once? Can you stop bothering me, for once?"

He stopped to speak with the mother.

They commiserated on how the summer was coming to an end. He wished her and the girl to have a nice evening.

He was walking away and heard them negotiating. "I am not going anywhere and don't be sassy with me. I am going to be here forever and forever and I'll be right here until you come inside and eat."

The daughter was laughing. "You are going to be there forever? There? Forever?" The mother laughed. Then the family where there was only the mother and her daughter went inside.

It was quiet but for the sound of his footsteps on the pavement.

So there was a family with whom he had had contact with, his old lost family, whose disloyal members had known who was and was not deserving. They had escaped one another's company. The grandmothers, grandfathers, fathers, mothers, brothers, sisters, aunts, uncles, daughters, sons, nephews and nieces had not been available to one another, as no one had thought to consider that there are reasons to be generous of heart and take care to be sure that everyone else was all right and to show a little concern.

He was coming up to the church. The front doors to it were open.

But the losses of an individual should not figure into what was what, if there is not a conclusion to come to, when remembering what was what, years later, when forgotten: the small-mindedness, cruelty, abandonment, reliance on bankrupt institutions, vanity, drunkenness, sentimentality, bullying, when forgotten. Then it is not useful to dwell on the past, in order to make excuses for the present, when keeping in mind that one version could be similar to another. But still a case is often made for misfortunes to be championed in order to justify the rights of the individual, so as to compensate each and every last man and woman for their unwavering unhappiness, and that despite the evidence that time-tested misery has always resisted every remedy and will do so regardless of efforts to right all wrongs.

There were parishioners at prayer inside the church. He could have gone inside to say hello to those he knew, to friends of the family and interrupted them in their prayers, or he might have entered unobserved and sat down and watched people pray, and that is a relaxing and idle way to pass the time: to wonder what it is that those who are devoted are praying for, and how little is known about that.

But to observe those observant in prayer was far from his mind, as he was after replenishing the devoured peaches that he had gobbled down the night before and that morning.

Mary-Adeline MacSweeney threw her door open for him.

In greeting each other they put aside concerns they should have had.

He told her how he was interested in getting more of her yellow-fleshed Cresthaven peaches. She thought that that must have been true and she promised him her orchard.

Then what was happening, what a hint of the intrigue was, in passing, they alluded to it. She mentioned the spouse's morning visit. They laughed.

So they were almost not sure who was talking at times, their statements where one started were finished by the other and what they were saying they repeated under their breaths and into each other's ears, and between their personalities there was just a slight separation.

Later the moon was shining in through the bedroom window. Later still, the late evening was coming to an early end.

— I only got here it seems like.

She invited him to stay for supper to eat the food she had intended to prepare for her guests, but he had to go and refuse another meal.

— What a shame.

She gave him a large bag of peaches, then as they were going by the apple trees down her driveway, they picked some apples, and they put the apples into the bag with the peaches and the hard fruit was rubbing up against the redolent tender soft fruit.

— Tomorrow?

— Tomorrow.

— I hope you sleep well.

— I shall.

He was walking back under the trees along the streets through the town, and he was enjoying a feeling of wanting to die for someone, but wanting to live for her, too. So he would have wanted to have gone back and to have enjoyed a fine gourmet meal and he might not have been sure why he had to go home, but his excuses he knew well. They were impossible to ignore.

The church was lit up in the moonlight. From out of the front door there was a glow of the interior light shining out onto the steps. The parishioners had left and gone home.

And on the other side of the building, in the small church cemetery, there was the minister standing amongst the headstones. He looked to be looking up at the heavens. Then what might have been a silent passing in the night, that caught their attention and called upon them to offer their mutual salutations.

— Are you having a nightly walk, Harold?

— I am.

— Heading home?

— I'm going that way.

— Well, I'm out here getting some fresh air and I'm looking for meteorites. There's supposed to be a shower of them tonight, but I haven't seen one yet. Also I'm enjoying a little wine, as I'm celebrating, no, I'm not celebrating. I'm commemorating, as tonight I'm closing the church up for good. Then today a friend said to me, "You're stepping down from your soapbox." I am, finally, I'm stepping down, after all these years.

He held up a wineglass.

— I'm sorry for that, George, he said to him.

— Everyone says they are and I think they mean it. And would

The Unorthodox Ox

you like to share in a glass of wine with me? To help me on my way and you on yours. I have a couple of bottles inside waiting to be drunk.

— I shouldn't really.

— It's good wine. I had been saving it for years, for this very night, I believe.

The minister stepped out from the graveyard.

— One glass, a toast, humour me if you can, if you would.

— One glass, all right.

They went up the front steps of the church.

— I consider it to be a demonstration of patience to age wine for your entire adult life and not lose your sense of taste before you can drink it.

They went inside and down the centre aisle.

From up above the dais light was shining down onto bottles of wine that were on the altar.

— You have to be impressed that you are about to taste a Chateau Léoville Las Cases 1982.

— I know nothing about it.

The minster was knowledgeable about the particularities of the domaine, the appellation, the vintage, the quality of the grapes that had gone into it, the time of maturation, what the changes were and how they occurred in the ageing process, and how wine merchants had maybe seen after what was necessary to insure the wine's long-term stability.

He poured a glass for him. He refilled his own glass.

— One of the perks of the profession that I appreciated was the wine I could drink. Then I got pleasure in talking about evil and entertaining sinners and those beyond redemption. But I don't recall you attending my services too often.

— Not since I was too young to remember.

— Your generation was hard to please. But you weren't one of those troubled in your youth, if I remember correctly.

— Only bored.

— Then could I or might I interest you in a sermon? I gave my best sermons when I had had a few. I know you're a nonbeliever. I like a challenge.

— It's too late for me now, George.

— It is never too late, never too late. And I never refuse an offer to speak if invited to. So I have sermons that deal with the usual sins, and depending on the purpose they vary in their severity. I'd be happy to carry forth, if you'd like to bear with me and hear me out, if you can. My usual approach to what it was that I spoke about was to provide strong counter-arguments, and sometimes, those were stronger than the point I wanted to make, for example, if condoning crimes like theft in situations when justifiable and there was no other option. I'd argue the wrong option, and I had to fight my way back to the right one and that was a challenge. Then I've sermons on the subjects of not bearing false witness against others, not robbing from the blind, except when absolutely necessary, not coveting a neighbour's wife, except when necessary, and one sermon, one sermon on the subject of murder, which is a topic few address with conviction. Because the belief is, is that someone who comes into a house of God would not have committed murder, but I suspect there are a few in the pews on any Sunday who may have killed someone or wanted to, or the odd repentant soldier. They are the first to get down on their knees. It's the only reason they were there. My audiences when I said this, the look of surprise on their surprised faces. And so I speculated on the lives that such people lead. I spoke about the communities that violence erupts from. I would bring up the motivations there are that lead one to committing violent criminal acts: greed and poverty. And I would say anyone can kill if you want to and or need to. Because it's simply a matter of thinking you're God. That's all that's to it. Then it's when we start to think we're God that we're really sinning. So what would you think if I told you I thought I was God? That I had killed someone? What would you think if you were to discover that a minister you've known for years was a hired gun who thought he was God, and from time to time liked to imbibe to excess? And there have been men of the cloth who weren't as high-minded as they might have been, could have been, should have been. So who can we trust? If it could be men like you or me? Who can we trust?

— No one probably.

— Can we trust ourselves?

— I don't think so.

— But if we can't trust ourselves, who is there to trust in this

The Unorthodox Ox

world? So there was my congregation asking that question that I put to them: "who can we trust?" Then in the meanwhile I would call out from my pulpit for Satan to come up from hell on the steam of all the evilness there must be there and for the figurative embodiment of Lucifer to ascend to our world and drive us off the road of righteousness, to prove a point, you see, that I could be right about everyone else being wrong. I used to scare myself.

— I had heard you got carried away at times.

— But who doesn't want to play with evil from time to time? Because we are interested in entertaining its possibilities. They are interesting the possibilities that evil offers, and it's irresistible for some not to entertain such possibilities, hard to say no to those unholy enticements. Then some of them were good sermons and I put a lot into them when I was starting out, but after a while I found I was having trouble being honest, and if we can't trust ourselves. But how far to go with the truth is a hard subject to get a handle on. I've never come to a conclusion about what the truth is, what the absolute truth is. Excuse me, this is what happens when I've had too much to drink, I can't hold my tongue, it runs away on me, wags away in my mouth like the tail of a dog who's happy to see his master.

The pastor poured another glass for himself.

— So now this church is being torn down. It didn't have to be. But it would have been expensive to repair was the excuse not to save it. Though had repair work been done when it had to be. The problems could have been solved inexpensively. I had informed those who would listen as to what the restoration was that had to be done. There was no interest, no money. Now it will cost more to tear it down than it would have to fix, and would you like to see the problem? I can show it to you. We'll have to go outside.

They went back outside and around the building into the cemetery, and the minister pointed at a crack in the foundation. Light was coming up out of it as if from hell itself.

— But cheers to all that is damned.

They clinked glasses and emptied them.

— I'm glad you like the wine. It was four hundred dollars a bottle, from money I stole from the offering plate. You see, we are all capable of evil. Would you like some more?

— I can't say no.

— You will have some more. It is good wine, isn't it?

They were coming out of the cemetery and back around to the front of the building when from down the street a voice called out.

— There you are, George. You are paying your respects to a friend or someone you once knew and at this time of night?

— Good evening, Trudi. Are you well? Hello.

— As ever, and you?

Ms. Trudi Brown rode up on a bicycle to the church steps.

— I am well, thank you, no, I wasn't paying my respects to anyone, maybe I should have.

— Pay them to me then, she said.

— I always do.

She rang a bell on the handlebars to happily announce her arrival.

— You thought I wasn't coming? She asked.

— I never would have doubted you were coming.

— Hello Harold, she said.

She dismounted from her bicycle. He greeted her in return.

— Then Trudi, you've noticed the luminous moon we have tonight for the occasion, George said to her.

— I have. And I see you're drinking out here for all to see. That is somewhat disgraceful.

— Yes, but I've been disgraced for years.

— You have been. That is no excuse. You need to think of a better one.

— Then I was just showing him the crack in the foundation, and would you like to see it, too? Because at times we have to see things to believe them, yet even that is sometimes not enough.

— No, no need for me to see it.

— And I was also telling him about my sermons.

— Of course, you were.

— Despite being an Irish Catholic, Trudi attended my services religiously, he said to him.

— That wasn't why I attended, she said.

— I gave a compelling sermon on murder, did I not? Was it not memorable?

— It was memorable, she replied.

The Unorthodox Ox

— I kept you up at night fearing for your own life?
— You kept me up.
— There were those who had trouble sleeping, who experienced fear from my fearful discourse.
She said then.
— And Harold, last night you gave me a fright yourself. I saw you in front of your house when riding by. I didn't want to say hello and put you on the spot.
— I wondered if it might have been you. Yes, my wife mentioned you had seen me.
— She did, fancy that, did she? Because she didn't believe me when I told her I had seen you. George, you wouldn't have believed it. This respectable man was in front of his house in the early morning going about as he came into the world in a state of undress, which is almost as reprehensible as your inebriated behaviour. I mentioned it to his new wife. I shouldn't have. I guess I don't know why I did. It was none of my damn business. But she thought there was no percentage to it. She let on that I had a few too many screws loose that I was out of my mind.
— Trudi, there is nothing wrong with being a little touched, nothing wrong with that, that I'm aware of.
— There is not unless you are wrongly being accused of it. And don't you know what it is to be wrongly accused?
— I believe to be touched is to be blessed by a divine spirit. And Trudi, if you've not already had too much maybe you'd like to partake in some spirits. I should like to offer you a glass of wine that I've blessed for our consumption.
— I wouldn't care if it is blessed or if it wasn't.
— I can unbless it for you if you like. I'll curse it if you like.
— Wouldn't I like something to drink?
She stood her bicycle up. They went into the church and down the aisle up to the altar. He spoke to her about the wine. He poured her a glass.
— Then do you remember what happened to us in 1982? Do you remember 82? George asked her.
In one draught she drank down the wine. She held the glass out for him to refill it.
— I remember 1982. How would I forget?

— You might want to drink it for its taste.
— For its taste, its taste? You do that?
— Tonight I am.
— Pour me another glass because I might want to forget 1982, George.

She downed the second glass and asked he immediately refill it.

— I was to have changed my faith for you on your account! she bellowed. Her voice echoed in the church.
— No, I don't think so. I wouldn't have asked that, I don't think.
— You would have. You would have asked that. There wasn't anything you wouldn't have asked me for.
— I am not one to argue with people about their religion. It's against my religion to do so.
— There was nothing that was against your religion, George. You may not have had one most of the time. You preached more nonsense than sense. You know you did.
— I did what I had to in order to be heard.
— Did I ever hear what I wanted to hear? You think I heard what I wanted to hear? Do you?
— I did what I had to, to get my point across so that some might know better than to harm others.
— But you went around doing harm yourself.
— I admit I did.
— Not to me you admitted it. You never admitted that to me. Did you admit that to me even once?!
— I should have. I should have. I know I should have.
— You know that? Do you? Really now!

She held her glass out to him again though it was not empty.

— Fill it up, all the way up to the brim, she demanded.
— But tonight can we not let bygones be bygones? he asked.
— I don't think so. Why would I?
— Can't we for once?
— Harold, George and I were close friends and he didn't think anyone wanted to know about us or should have known. What a goddamn hypocrite!
— But we are all hypocrites. There is no man alive who is not prone to that weakness.
— 'We are all hypocrites and prone to it.' Say it again and I'll

The Unorthodox Ox

believe you for once.

She laughed with good humour, but from a perspective of disappointed resignation.

— Trudi, you must be civil or I'll have a mind to ask you to leave the premises.

— You're going to toss me out on my arse from your condemned church? She guffawed.

— I wouldn't want to.

— You always invited me in though.

— I'd ask you to leave if I had to. I would.

— You were always inviting me in. It didn't matter when or where, and you couldn't ask me to leave even if you wanted to.

The two old lovers spoke about what they would have done. They welcomed him to eavesdrop.

Then the more they drank, the more they confessed their minor sins to each other, and they were recreating some of the adventure, the youthful magic from when he had been a young and idealistic pastor and she a bonny Irish immigrant full of a discernible love for life's pleasures that had been so unkindly influenced by centuries of cruel and guilt-ridden tradition.

How they were remembering what they were looking back upon from years ago.

— When I think of how much I missed you all the time, how you made me suffer, she said.

— I know, I know, he said.

They lit candles on the altar. They were opening another bottle of wine. They were looking further back into almost forgotten distant regrets.

Then without them noticing he slipped out the front door of the church, and they would not have noticed his leaving for some time, so far gone were they and how far all would have led those two old people, he himself would not have wanted to have witnessed.

§

He climbed up to stand on his tree stump.

Then he was going over rules of grammar and how syntax works, thereby concluding that a means for expression was in order, but the thoughts themselves. *What indulgence, as if a man is anything other than someone as expressed by words and the known rules of language. I'm not wrong to think so. No. But who am I talking to? Myself as my only witness?*

Coming from out the back-door and into the yard came Karol. He did not know how she knew he was there. Because of his muttering out loud.

She got up to stand on her stump. They looked at each other and out into the field.

— Where did you go?

— I went for a little walk.

— Did you have a good walk?

— Yes. I went further than I realized. It took me some time to walk back.

He showed her the bag with the hard and soft fruit in it.

— Mary-Adeline MacSweeney was out when I went by. I got us more fruit. It's ripe and has to be eaten.

— I ate already.

— I was hoping you weren't waiting for me.

— Not by now I wouldn't be.

— That's what I was hoping.

She looked back over her shoulder into the yard.

— I see you didn't do the yard work.

— I can't do it in the dark.

— You might turn on the yard light.

— That would disturb the neighbours.

— Is something wrong? What is wrong with you?

— Nothing's wrong. I'm thinking is all.

— Thinking about what, are you thinking, Harold?

— I'm thinking about the funeral I'm going to tomorrow. I'm getting myself in the mood for it.

A falling star flew over them.

— Also I was thinking about scientific matters, and so I was reminded of a quote by Jules Poincaré, who said, 'A scientist does not study nature because it is useful.' That's not always why. 'He studies it because he delights in it and he delights in it because it's beautiful.' Then beauty is to be admired someone ugly said to me once. Now was Mr. Poincaré ugly? I can't remember if he might have been. I have no idea what he looked like.

The wine had had an effect on him.

— There goes a shooting star. Did you see it? she asked him.

He had not.

— That means we are going to be lucky, she said.

— We'll have to wait and see about that, but I somehow doubt it. I doubt it, Karol, that we will be lucky, you and I.

— There is to be a shower of them tonight I heard.

But the only star of the night that he could have seen had fallen.

— 'Is it nature in human nature that makes us human?' I don't remember who it was who asked that. I can't for the life of me remember who asked that.

— I don't know either. I'm going inside then.

— I'll watch for falling stars. I am not too tired at the moment. Sleep well, he said to her.

Then leaving behind whatever else had been left unsaid she went inside. She went upstairs.

He waited until he saw the bedroom light go off and he went in, but he did not go up to bed as he had thought he would have wanted to read over some of his notes, his papers (from his studies) that were on the subjects of *statistical dispersion*, *qualitative variation*, *box plots*, and also on *information entropy*, tools for measuring uncertainty. And he went over some of the known processes for the unwinding of the somewhat visible universe, and it was as he was considering the size and mass of things and what proportionate correlations meant, that without him realizing it the meteorites of the night fell in a shower of light.

§

In the morning he was leaving and stepping out the door. She stopped him in his tracks.

— You think you're going to a funeral looking like that? You think you can go to a funeral like that? Have you seen yourself? Look at you. Wait there.

She went into the house and came back out with a lint brush, then the suit, his mourning attire, she brushed to remove loose threads, lint, dust, and hair.

— I can't understand why it is a point of pride for you to be so slovenly. You're shameless. And last night you didn't brush yourself before you got in bed, though now I'm asking you to. I know you didn't.

She clawed away at the brush for what she had scraped off him.

— Look at the crap and the shit on you, Harold. Then I shouldn't say you're shameless. You're just shameful.

— You don't want to deny me my shame, Karol. Please, don't take that away from me.

She showed him again what she had removed and would have wanted to have rubbed the tip of his nose in it maybe. Then she told him she would not want to be caught dead in his company even at a funeral. She forced herself to laugh loudly.

— Have the time of your life, and you'll be talking shop with your work colleagues, no doubt.

— It is a working funeral. That's right.

— Harold, you know, I'm not always amused by those kinds of quips and remarks.

— You are not always amused. No, you're not. Then I thank you for brushing my suit.

He turned around for her to see if she was satisfied. She muttered a few words in disgust. She went into the house.

Then when he had said that he was going to the funeral, he had been looking to get out of having to go out and to amuse her and to monitor frogs and so for him to attend the funeral had just popped out.

Later, it had occurred to him then, that he and Mary-Adeline could take advantage of what the opportunity afforded. So the night before they had decided that they would meet that next day and they would spend the day together. They had planned for a picnic lunch, if it was not raining, or they would have made other arrangements if the weather was inclement.

But he had time on his hands before they were to meet for lunch. Of course, going to the funeral in the meantime was not a possibility.

Then he thought that he would go out and drive aimlessly around for a while, although driving around is not an altogether aimless pursuit, as drivers follow the roads that direct the aimlessness of a man's wandering desires, yet, however, regardless, there still is freedom to indulge in and to enjoy for drivers at the wheel who are being guided along to go where they may have been before and they're happy that they recognize the road they are on, or if it is a distinctly different road they're pleased that it is similar to what is so familiar about many roads; i.e., the width and the forward distance lying ahead, the smooth and even surfaces or the predictable or surprising location of imperfections, but he was not necessarily pleased in that sense as he started out to drive around and not altogether aimlessly.

He arrived and took up a pair of binoculars that he had. He got out of his car and set off on a footpath into what was the nearby woods. He came to a dry river-bed that the path dropped down into, he followed the dry river-bed, climbing over fallen branches. He avoided stagnant pools of water. He stepped over garbage and rotting materials that had been left behind by the receding waters after the storm. Beneath the leaves of overhanging trees air was motionless and stale with ambient decomposition, and the time it took as he went along immersed him in an unpleasantness that got worse before improving. Then the air began to stir and through the trees a lake came into sight. He came out of the woods and out onto a pebbled beach.

The lake was in a nature reserve. It was as it had always been, in its original natural state. There were no houses along its shores nor motorized waterborne traffic. The body of water was teaming with aquatic and ecstatic life.

He was to walk along the lake shore, and he found what he was looking for: the torn-down and broken-up fence and the uprooted sign that read *Piping Plovers - Pluvier Siffleur (Charadrius Melodus) Breeding Grounds, Lieu de reproduction.*

The site had been vandalized before the Piping Plovers had nested. There were no Piping Plovers nesting.

The destruction, he would report it. He made note of what was important to determine.

He went back down into the river-bed. He retraced his coming that was as unpleasant as before, and it was as he was going along that he was looking for other tell-tale signs that might have been important. There were none.

Back at his car he looked out through his binoculars to see if there was anything else that needed his attention and he happened to spot a pair of Boreal Chickadees sitting in a tree. Then it was unusual to see such a rare breed of Chickadee; sightings were few and far between in the region. Several years had gone by since he might have remembered having seen a Boreal Chickadee.

He got in his car and he drove to where they were to meet, arriving an hour earlier than the agreed time. But moments afterwards Mary-Adeline arrived as well.

— You do look as if you have almost come from a funeral, she said to him.

— Yes, I'm cleverly disguised as someone in mourning. It worked well. I only had a little trouble getting out of the house.

— And we're early.

— We are.

— I wanted to make sure I had extra time in case I got lost, she said.

— We didn't want to be late. I'm glad you didn't get lost.

— So am I.

They were looking forward to a lot, but not asking for too much of anything out of consideration.

— It is strange to be this early. There was no way I could have got lost? she asked.

— Not for long.

It was unusual that he was dressed for a funeral, that they had arrived early. It was curious that he had come from seeing the destruction of the Piping Plover nesting grounds. There was the sighting of Boreal Chickadees, how strange.

— We're surprised, she said.

— Yes.

— Then this morning I played some music in a way in which I had never played it, and to play differently what I know well, was unusual for me. I was amazed.

It was the initial beginning stage of it all.

— If we stop at nothing? he asked her.

It was from off the outside of an aerostat. They untied weights from the hot-air balloon's basket and the inflated balloon rose up on a current of rising air. It sailed out over the ocean. In the water below were sharks. The balloon fell towards the water, blown down by a gust of wind. There were shark fins circling in the sea. A stronger gust blew the balloon back upwards. They rose on the updraught. The fish in the water rolled onto their backs. They opened their mouths. Offal poured out. The sea was a cloudy red.

— What is it? We should ask who are we to doubt anything? Who are we to doubt anything? he asked.

They were unreservedly taking into consideration whatever doubts there were. Wondering all about them from every last angle. Maybe.

Then if a day would come when they would somehow fly away somewhere in a hot-air balloon and with no absolute destination in mind.

But perhaps it follows that details, minutiae, can change the significance of about anything and everything. Then about anything and everything becomes forever momentous, just about and almost. A single out of place loose strand of hair, it becomes a memory for the idea that that thread of hair is modestly and discernibly rooted into, and it is in art maybe, similarly as it is when hopelessly in love, that by slowing down time that that characterizes what are memorable moments for a kind of arbitrary sort of man or woman of that kind who cannot afford to wait around to be in love, not forever.

They were talking about impressions, their experiences, what came up, not ignoring worries. She told him stories about teachers she had had and her early mentors. She said to him that she had always wondered who her audiences were in fact, and it worried her sometimes that they always demanded she keep on performing and never stop. Though there was the music.

He pointed then at the greenery that was around them and at what would hopefully never fail if a decision were to be made not to destroy everything in the natural world, assuming that the making of such a decision would be enough and that it was not too late.

— More than anything we shouldn't have to believe that we have to expect that the worst has yet to happen, he said, we shouldn't have to expect that.

It was supposed to have rained, but the weather was co-operating. The clouds in the sky avoided blocking the sun.

They found a spot for their picnic and lay a blanket down up from the banks of the river. They sat down. They had an open view of the water and fields around them. The food she had brought she got out.

— I marvelled at your vegetables when I met you the first time. Now I know that that wasn't the half of it.

— What I gave you was as fresh as could be.

She lay the food out on the blanket.

— It looks fresh.

— Picked this morning. You'll like what's on the menu.

— I promise I will.

— I hope so.

— It looks delicious.

— I'm glad you will like it.

— I think I will.

— You wouldn't tell me if you don't.

— No.

— But I will know.

— That seems like a promise of some kind, and it is promising to make promises.

— It is.

They ate lunch.

Then neither of them was hoping or expecting that the worst could happen, not then or hopefully never, anything but.

But then what occurred was not as it was or must have even seemed.

It was from up the river, behind and from around a bend, a rowboat was coming down, it drifted by in front of them. In the small one-person boat, a boatman was standing unsteadily, he was rocking the little boat. The boatman held up a camera. He gestured to them to get their permission to take a picture. They smiled for the picture. The boat drifted away on the current down the river.

High above them an air-plane was flying slowly against the expanding backdrop of the clouds. An early autumn leaf was blowing around before them, it fell into the river. The strand of hair hanging over her forehead he pushed aside. It fell back down. He pushed it back up.

They were saying other things and making inspirational pronouncements.

Nearby was a gathering of birds having an animated conversation over hotly disputed territory.

Then from down-river the boatman came rowing back up against the current. He brought his boat to shore and he beached it. The intruder got out of his boat. He took several pictures of them.

The plane was picking up speed. Another leaf fell into the water. The plane shot over the horizon. The boatman wished the two of them to have a pleasant day and a long and prosperous life. Again the man floated off.

Whatever else happened was to remain forever materially a long-standing mystery.

She got out the dessert and asked him to close his eyes and not even think of peeking.

— I don't know how to peek. I am not good at peeking.

And without thinking of opening his eyes he savoured a chocolate truffle that she dropped into his mouth. He licked her fingers clean of melted chocolate, and they fed each other chocolates and other ideas, one idea at a time, one chocolate, another one.

They were revealing other secrets to each other that no one in their right mind would have shared with anyone.

The afternoon had been theirs. The night would also be.

— I'll be home waiting for you. Come early if you can, she said to him.

— I will, yes, I will.

A horse in a field whinnied.

He followed her in his car. At the end of her driveway he stopped. He watched her drive up between the apple trees to her house. He waited for her to get out and go inside. From the door, before she went in, she waved to him and she blew him a kiss.

He drove on home.

§

There was a note at home that informed him that that evening he was to attend supper at his mother-in-law's.

Harold, I went out and I was going to call you in the afternoon, but I saw you left your phone at home. You didn't want to take it with you to the funeral, that's understandable, I suppose. But you could have turned it off. So Helen is expecting us at seven. I will see you then, at supper, Dear.

The note also had instructions for what he was to take care of in the meanwhile, if he would.

His papers on entropy that were lying about, she was hoping that he would pick them up; and he attempted to put them in order, within the bounds of the subject itself. Then while he was doing so he came across a book that she had been reading, a happy-ever-after romance, and so she was following adventures in a book that judging by its cover would have been written by a second-rate hack. He must have thought better than to shelve it where it might not have belonged.

He went out to look after the yard work, because if he had not done so:

Should we just let the yard go to seed? Or we could leave the gate to the field open? How would you like cattle wandering into the yard to graze? You would have to look after picking up their paddies. You'd have to scoop up the cow-pies. Would you want to have to do that? You wouldn't, I know you wouldn't. Don't try to argue that you would. I know you wouldn't, and don't try to pretend otherwise, damn you.

Then in the yard he saw how the bird feeder was empty, seedless. That was troubling, because not to provide a reliable food supply is stressful for birds who depend on food from a feeder. Even a brief disruption can be fatal for the older and younger ones. In honesty he had to be careful and not become too distracted due to recent events and lose his wits completely.

He filled the feeder and he went inside, and with remorseful satisfaction he watched hungry birds fly in and after the first rush, he went back out and retrieved the glass that had been left on his tree stump.

Back inside he sat in the living room to watch runs on the feeder as aggressive species made way for less aggressive ones. And staring out the window into the early evening he was sitting gloomily in the gloaming, thinking about his own ingenuity and whether it would let him down or lift him up to great heights.

Then perhaps it would have been to distract himself from whatever else he had to do, he got up and he went down into his private space in the basement, and he opened the door panels to the display cases on the walls that housed his insect collection; he had a fine collection for what was its size and its content, if compared to larger collections as are found in natural history museums, especially for the varieties of beetles and of the butterflies. The specimens in their cases were displayed and laid out by their order, genus, species, name, and in pairs, but not all matched. And there were open slots that he had to fill. Particularly for what were several of the Ruteline beetles that he had an appreciation for because of their colourful and exotic markings. Then it had been from when he had started collecting specimens of the different varieties of Ruteline beetles that there was one of the unique Rutelines that he had hoped to get his hands on, the prized Madecacesta Gaudroni Ruteline of Madagascar, so he had made a pact with himself, a promise, fanciful as it was, to go to Madagascar to catch a female Madecacesta Gaudroni. But when and how was the problem, as is the case with one's remotest dreams. He was looking at the empty slot in the display case for a few moments.

Then there was outside of the main collection, a Ruteline beetle pinned to a lampshade. It was a beetle broach, a Ruteline beetle glued on to a lapel pin. It had been a living beetle stuck to a pin that once he had made a present of to Karol. She had refused it, and she had been repulsed by the bug squirming on the broach that he had wanted to pin over her heart.

He unpinned the broach. He put it in his pocket. He closed the door panels to his insect collection.

He went to his mother-in-law's for supper.

There were phone messages that he did not listen to.

§

They were seated at the table and had not been intending to wait much longer for him to arrive to begin the meal. He let himself in. He excused himself to them for his having lost track of the time.

Then Karol told him that she was displeased and unhappy that he had not let her know that he was going to be so late. Also she was annoyed that he had not bothered to change out of his mourning attire that he was still wearing.

— Look at you, I married a misanthrope. I don't know what to do with you. Harold, what am I supposed to do with you? What am I supposed to say to you?

— You'll think of something, Karol.

— If I don't?

— You will no doubt.

He asked they forgive his appearance, and to excuse his not having changed into what would have been more suitable apparel he described to them what would have been a version of his attendance at the funeral. He told them how the emotional outpouring had gone on for an extended time. He related that family and friends had been undone. He gave them what would have been an accurate description of the heart-wrenching grieving of certain individuals. He mentioned the deceased woman's comely appearance.

— The eulogy wasn't as well written as it could have been.

Helen thought to ask what was the cause of death of the poor deceased girl.

— It would have had to have been unexpected, what anything that's like that is like, he said.

— I don't understand the comparison you're making, Karol said to him.

— I don't know what the cause was. I didn't ask. She was young. She had her whole life ahead of her.

He sat down at the table.

— Hopefully nothing like that happens to us and we have to look after ourselves, exercise, eat right, and mind our own business, said Helen.

— We do.

— Though I'm the first to admit that there is a point of no return as to how old we can get before we're a burden, before I will become a burden. Then I hope I won't become a burden to you. It's bad enough to get old without becoming a stone around the neck of those who have to care for you. You'll have to forgive me if you end up taking care of me when you will have better things to do.

— You could never be a burden, Harold said to her.

— I might be.

— We would tell you if you were.

— Do not let me burden you and don't burden your own children either. Don't do that.

— We won't, he said.
— Then Harold can you tell me how my knives are? I got them sharpened recently, and don't cut yourselves.
— You remembered I told you to get them sharpened, Mother.
— It was you who told me to get them sharpened?
— Who else would have?
— It was good of you to tell me to do so.

Then it was the right time, as much as another, to call their attention as to why they were having supper together, Karol's reason why.
— Well, I'm afraid to make my own announcement, I am, and I'll let you speak on my behalf, she said to him.
— What's that? Your announcement? he asked her.
— He's going to be my proxy, Mother, she said.
— Who? she asked.
— My misanthropic husband.

He understood then what Karol meant.
— He will be my spokesman, my representative, for the moment, and speak on my behalf, if you would like to. You've always wanted to. For the time being, of course.
— For how long? he asked her.
— Just for now, Harold.
— Then Helen, I believe she wants me to tell you that she has a new contract, which is going to be for the design of a correctional institution. But I can't tell you too much, as I don't know how much I ought to say. I had been instructed to say nothing to anyone, and for how long I didn't know.
— A contract? Helen asked.
— Then I hear by your tone of voice that you disapprove, and you didn't say you objected before, Karol said to him.
— What's it for though? Helen asked.
— It's a correctional facility, a penitentiary, he said to her.
— You object now, do you? Karol asked him.
— I don't object, he said.
— You didn't say anything to me before. And I assumed you didn't think it was a problem, but it is. I know that. I've my concerns. That's what I was telling you, that's what we were discussing for God's sake.
— A correctional facility? Helen asked.

— It's industrial work is what it is, she said to her.

They started in on the meat they were to eat.

— I know why one would object.

— I don't object, and if I didn't before, I wouldn't do so now, he said.

He commented on the knives.

— The knives are sharp. The meat is tender, Helen.

— Yes, I accidentally cut myself.

— It's a one-time contract, Karol said.

Then to defuse what was beginning to become an escalating and possible inevitable argument, Helen commented.

— Certainly, it's unfortunate that there are those individuals who have to be kept out of harm's way. But I imagine there's no sensible option but to take care of such people in the only way available. Although more has to be done for those who get themselves into trouble. But how can we help a person who is not fit to mingle with those of us who might want to help them?

They were eating.

— Then the latest news is that I'm going away next week. I am to start consulting, I found out today. I am to meet with contractors, Karol said.

She said where she was going.

— That's the third world? asked Helen.

— Yes, but they don't like to call it that themselves.

Then she told them that regardless of her own and anyone's legitimate objections that the project was going to be interesting for a number of reasons and why that maybe was.

He added.

— Well, I think that if one were to object that an issue to take into consideration is that there are instances when we all deserve a second chance in life before having to serve time behind bars, but it is hard to be forgiving in certain instances.

— What are you saying now?

— I'm adding that as an aside.

— That's not the issue, Karol said.

— Under certain circumstances it could be, he said.

— That's not my concern.

— Maybe not.

The Unorthodox Ox

They let whatever else there was to argue pass.

Then it was an appropriate or just as well the right moment to make another announcement that was on behalf of others as well.

— Monday morning, you know that the church is going to be torn down. It's going to be a public event. People will be coming in from elsewhere to watch the demolition. We should attend maybe, he said.

— Goodness gracious me, so many churches have been torn down, said Helen wistfully.

— And prisons are being built to replace them, he said.

— I did know about it. But I don't know if I would want to go, Helen said.

— There will be people you know who will be there, Helen.

— There will be, but I don't know if I want to be there.

— You'll see people you haven't seen in a while.

— I want to see most of them?

Then in reference to the church demolition that brought up the topic of the gatherings that had taken place there. What had been: autumn fairs, bake sales, corn roasts, strawberry socials, turkey tombolas, coffee klatsches, quilting bees, raffles, weddings and funerals, and what had been events in the lives of the members of the diminishing congregation.

— I remember the old days and there will not be many others like them, Helen said.

She spoke about her recollections.

They finished the meal. They were ready to leave. They stepped outside.

— It hasn't started to rain yet, he observed.

— Fine, all right, I'll be there Monday morning to see the catastrophe, she said to them.

There was lightening. They were walking home.

— You have to object, and you could have said so before. If it isn't one thing it's always another. It always is with you, she said.

— I don't mind and you know I can be indifferent when I want to be, he said.

— What kind of comment was that? Prisons are being built to replace them. You know that was uncalled for. It was a smug remark, Harold.

— You might think that because you don't know what kind of comment it is with me.

— I don't seem to, but I do, she sighed.

They were home. He said he would stay outside. He wanted to take a walk.

— It's about to rain.

— I'll come running back if it does, Karol.

— Do as you please then. Do I care? I don't care. I should know I shouldn't care.

He walked back past his mother-in-law's. He came up to the church, where there he stopped to look over what had been done in preparation for the demolition.

The graves in the cemetery had been dug up. Tombstones and caskets carted away. Off of the exterior of the building moulding had been stripped off. Leaning up against the outside walls of the building were doors and window frames. And looking in through the front door-frame he would have imagined that the dark interior was vastly empty and that the altar and the pews had been removed and hauled off to a landfill.

He went on.

He presented to Mary-Adeline the beetle broach. He asked for her permission to pin it over her heart.

Then to explain himself in some way perhaps, he recounted the creationist story of the dung-beetle that had come down from the distant past and was relevant to the present and the future.

— Although this is a Ruteline beetle, and if it were a dung-beetle that would be a magnificent coincidence, as dung-beetles played a part in brightening up the world; the dung-beetle was mythologically responsible for rolling the sun across the sky during the day to bring light to the world. She was a symbol of hope and rebirth. But a Ruteline beetle is more decorative than a dung-beetle, as you can see.

She accepted the gift. He pinned it over her thumping heart.

— I've come with news, he said.

He told her that Karol was going away for a week and that in the future she would likely be going away on frequent trips. So she was not going to be around to cause so many problems.

— This could not have come at a better time for her to have to go away and get out of my hair.

— Oh, I would like to apologize for how complicated things might be for you. But I'm not sorry. And if there is anything I could do to make matters worse for you, I might like to think so.

— You must be reading my mind, because I was wondering, I was thinking. I've an idea of going away on a trip. I'm hoping you might be interested to go on a trip? You and I. A trip north?

— A trip you say?

— It's a nice area, far north, where there is not a living soul for miles. It is a remote and a wild region in the north country.

— It sounds like it. I could be interested. I could be.

— You are?

— We could go on a trip?

— I didn't know what you'd think of the idea and on such short notice. It could be for the week? While she is gone.

— I like the idea. I'm interested.

— I was hoping you might like it.

— But come with me now then.

She led him to her practice studio and she sat him down, and she was to play for him a piece for which she had made her re-interpretive choices.

Then in that private performance, there was that same quality that he had heard in the recording for what was the sensitivity and the refined precision of her playing, and when and after she broke what were the beginning opening chords into their parts, there were choices for him as the listener to make on how to follow the intertwining lines of notes as they moved out into his consciousness and into silence.

Then when after she had finished the final recapitulating theme, he was looking at her with his eyes full of gratitude and with feelings of awe and reverence and with a sense of humility that would have inspired a God to tip his hat and throw it to the wind. This was the feeling that overcame him.

She gave him an account of her interpretation, and what she was saying to him had to do with the dedicated years of practising and playing and asking and answering many questions.

They went outside. They were walking in the cool fresh night air. They entered a hot-house where over the rows of the beds of peat moss the light delicate leaves of fruit trees were floating and fluttering from rising heat from the peat moss. Not high in the sky above the hot-house a night-hawk was flying, cawing, but that was not apparent to them as they found themselves to be snuggling into their assurances. They took note of nothing else.

Were he to have made off with more fruit that might have aroused suspicion at home, so he gorged himself before leaving.

Then had it taken longer for them to say goodbye, their parting would have exaggerated the difficulty of it. He was lingering. They were to see each other before they knew it.

— I'd like for you to stay the night.

— I am finding it hard to leave.

— But you better go?

He dragged himself away with what was the reminiscence of irrepressible and unbridled yearning.

When he was going by the church a cat crossed his path. A dog barked somewhere in another faraway neighbourhood.

The light was on in their upstairs bedroom.

— She's still up, of course, he heard himself muttering to no one in particular other than himself. He was looking up towards the light in the bedroom window for as long as he was to do so. He then decided that he was not able to bring himself to go inside right away and climb the stairs, shower, maybe brush his skin, and get into bed and say "Good night Karol, pleasant dreams, I love you more than anyone."

He walked on and he went out of the town along on a field service road, but with nowhere to go when he came to the end of it he turned around and headed slowly back home.

He could have done some yard work or found maybe what else there was to do, but he was tired. It was starting to rain. He went inside, climbed the stairs, he undressed and showered. He slipped into bed. He turned off the light, but she woke up when he turned it off. She was almost alarmed. He had to have startled her.

— So I was reading and fell asleep. Then this book is keeping me up, still I fell asleep. I would like to find out what will happen in the inane story.

— I would like to know what's going to happen, too, he said.

She turned on the light to put her book away.

The Unorthodox Ox

— Is that intended to be an insult, Harold? Are you trying to insult me? I'm half asleep and you're waking me to insult me?
— It was an insult to myself.
— To yourself?
— That was my intention.
She appeared to ignore his intention.
— The story makes me feel as if I had almost lived it myself.
— Maybe you have.
— That is an insult.
— Yes.
— You don't want me to go away, I know. That's your objection, isn't it?
— I want you to go away, if it is what you want to do.
— You would like me to feel guilty for having to go off to do what I have to do to earn a living.
— I'm the one who is guilty, Karol.
— I'm being paid well.
— I don't object.
— I'd rather you didn't.
— Not at all.
— I don't know if you're being sincere.
— I am sincere. That's one of my faults.
— Of many.
— I want you to do what you want to do to make a living no matter what it is.
— I intend to.
She turned away from him.
— You went for a long walk.
— I must have.
— Where did you go?
— I went down to the river.
— It doesn't seem to be raining hard.
— Not yet. No.
Then he thought to smooth over any ruffled feathers.
— When I went by the church cemetery I saw they had dug it up, and the graves have been left open. They should have filled them in. Someone who might want to pay their respects to a loved one could fall into an open hole.

— God forbid.
— And hurt themselves.
— You're worried about it?
— I'm telling you.
— If you were worried about it you should have filled them in.
— No, I don't think it would be up to me to fill in graves, not in the middle of the night. If someone saw me they could get the wrong idea. But they should have filled them in after they dug them up, one would think.

There was a lull.

— You think what I'm going to do is wrong? Don't you?
— I don't and I'm not sure what's right or wrong myself and we can't be right all the time in any case.
— After the preliminary work is done and when I stay down longer you can visit me.
— I could.
— I shouldn't worry about your objections nor my own?
— It would be best not to.
— I do object myself though. It's a large project. It worries me its size, how big it is going to be. They're going to expand the complex likely. They're talking of housing tens of thousands of inmates. It could end up being one of the largest complexes in the southern hemisphere.
— But you will be well taken care of and you will have servants who will wait on you hand and foot.
— Are you convincing me?
— I hope so.
— I am supposed to think that you are not always such a difficult person. I forget that at times.
— You remember it is not true.
— Then Harold, why didn't you tell me I had messages? You should tell me if I've messages. You know my reputation is based on being dependable and if it is someone else's fault that I'm not. I can't use that as a good excuse.
— You didn't call in to listen to them yourself? he asked.

He turned off the light. They were quiet.

— The messages were calls from people asking about the demolition, she said.

She was not finished.

— It's not only for the money. It is strategic for my career. Anyway, we do not have to reproach ourselves for what we have. And you'd object if I were helping the rich. You'd say I'd lost my ideals. But we don't want more than what we need.

— You'll find it interesting. You'll like the weather. You'll have a chance to see what it's like to have servants waiting on you.

— I could get used to that.

— You will.

— Then when I get back I will ask more of you.

— You'll do that.

— What would you do if I asked more of you?

— Whatever you would ask.

— You've convinced me of my own decision?

— You want me to say no.

— Tell me you'll miss me.

— You want me to say no.

— Tell me you'll miss me.

— I shall miss you.

— So then I should thank you for cleaning the house.

— It needed to be cleaned you said in your note. It was my pleasure.

— I will miss you, too. But you know, you still have to mow the lawn.

It was beginning to pour down outside.

§

It was raining in the morning. They went out in the rain for the morning and later for the evening monitoring of the frogs.

Then throughout the day she went over with him her decision for her work. She solicited his advice that he might have had to give. More calls came in from those inquiring about the demolition.

He had had to call Mary-Adeline to tell her he was not going to be able to get out of the house. They would see each other the next day they promised. They were dreaming about it as they spoke.

It rained that night. All night it rained. It was pouring down in the morning.

They dressed themselves for the weather to go out to watch the demolition.

Down along the streets people were going along towards the church.

Around the site barricades were holding back the arriving onlookers. At the front and at the sides of the building was demolition machinery. On hand were police constables who were making a showing of their professional training to reassure those who were perhaps fearful of what the world was becoming when a police presence is required for a church to be torn down.

Trudi Brown and the minister were sitting on the bench having a private conversation.

Behind the barricades workers were busy with their preparations.

The crowd for some time had been concerned about what was an ongoing delay. One man called out.

— Is this to be starting any time soon, Councillor? Do you know, if so, when?

Councillor Elrod was behind the barricades consulting with the workers.

Then there were spectators who took pause. They appeared to be weighing a subtlety not often thought of and that is unusual for crowds.

Other complaints for the demolition to begin arose.

— They're getting paid to be on strike? a woman demanded to know.

— Isn't it a private company doing the job? How can they be on strike? someone else asked.

A sergeant constable looked towards those individuals who were quiet when confronted with police scrutiny.

Harold was to make his way forward from out on the periphery. He greeted anyone he knew as he went. At the barricades he waved to Councillor Elrod to call him over to consult with him. The Councillor acknowledged the request to speak with a person who he knew held a related administrative position similar to his own.

— You've a restless crowd on your hands to contend with Councillor, Harold said.

— The conditions are slowing us up a little. But then we're not here to put on a show.

— Yet the crowd is here for the show. And you probably wouldn't deny you're interested in playing to the crowd. I would imagine you would not want to disappoint the public.

— That's why we're here, an onlooker interjected.

— We're taking necessary precautions.

— Then if I may, I would like to ask about how the consultations transpired for this, what the process was?

— We had consultations. There was a forum held.

— I didn't hear anything about consultations neither before nor after a decision was made.

— We accepted and reviewed written petitions as well.

— I didn't hear about a forum or about petitions either.

— If you are not a religious person you would not have been as interested as some.

— This is not only a religious matter.

— There were a number of considerations.

— A few years couldn't have been afforded to let the older generation move on?

— I'm afraid not.

— And I'd like to ask why the graves were dug up and not filled in and left like that?

— They will fill them in.

— You don't appreciate what it is like for surviving family members to see the graves of their relatives dug up, to see empty holes where their kin were peacefully resting? It demonstrates insensitivity, Councillor. You can imagine how they must feel to have to look at what can be considered to be a desecration.

— Yes, but they had to be dug up.

— You should have had the holes filled in at the least. There was no reason why you wouldn't have filled the holes immediately.

— It will be done when we are finished.

— You should have filled them in right away for pity's sake. You had to have filled the holes in as soon as you dug them up.

— We will do that.

— It was the sensitive and respectful thing to have done for Christ's sake. You had to have filled in the damn holes.

There was a roar from a motor, a throttling up of a diesel engine, the sound of wood breaking. The belfry tittered, it snapped and fell off the back of the building. There was a crash of wood splintering.

Amongst the crowd there were those who moved forward. Others stepped back. The constables were ready and alert. A small young child asked if there was anyone inside and was the person going to be all right? An elderly woman began praying out loud. The child was crying inconsolably.

The praying woman said.

— It's the beginning of the end of everything.

Councillor Elrod turned away to address a foreman who was calling out orders to the workers to prepare for what was next.

Harold went back through the crowd avoiding those he did not know well or whose names he might have forgotten, but he was detained on the way by a few to whom he said "It is a shame, it is."

Then in the meantime, Mary-Adeline had arrived, and when he saw that she was in conversation with Karol he passed by other people he might have spoken to. He made his way quickly.

— Hello, he said to her.

— Good morning, she said.

— How are you Mary-Adeline? he asked.

— I am well, thank you and you?

— Very well, thank you.

That was how they greeted one another.

Karol continued with what she was saying.

— People should try to understand that these quickly erected structures were originally intended to be only temporary. Then many have been torn down or destroyed in fires. Progress must go on. There's no way to stop it.

— You are right, there doesn't seem to be any way to stop progress, he said, not in any way wanting to necessarily challenge her.

— But you like the advantages that it offers us, as we all do, Karol said to him.

— But there are the disadvantages, and it's unfortunate that it always goes on without considering what are the disadvantages sometimes, he said.

— Of course, but nothing is perfect, she said.

The building's façade came down. The sidewalls fell inwards. The roof collapsed down into the foundation. The back outer wall fell backwards. Rain settled the dust that was rising. Other children were crying and being led away.

— It's upsetting for the children, said Mary-Adeline.

Helen then arrived.

— Look at what they have done and do you know how many of us got married in that church? And not just once, and the graves!

— It's a desecration, he said.

— I see why I didn't want to come.

Helen said hello to Mary-Adeline.

— You wish you hadn't come either, Miss, I bet. It looks like everyone here thinks that. Then there's George and Trudi making a thoroughly improper spectacle of themselves, how embarrassing for them and everyone else.

The noise of saws and hammering drove the crowd away.

He noticed that Mary-Adeline was wearing the beetle broach, it was not completely visible through the semi-opaque raincoat that she was wearing.

— So I haven't seen anyone who I knew, said Helen.

— I've met a few, he said to her.

They were moving further off from the commotion.

— This is what happens, what it's like when buildings are torn down. People get excited beforehand, and when it happens there's disappointment, said Karol.

— I wasn't excited, said Helen.

— Mother, you are better off to have been present than wish later you hadn't missed it. You'd have asked what happened afterwards if you hadn't come.

— I'd have asked what? I can't think of anything. It's a heap of rubble is what it is.

Then Mary-Adeline was to excuse herself. To take her leave.

— It's too bad. It was a nice church, she said to them.

— Of course, we know it wasn't one of the grand old European cathedrals, but it brought us together as a community. Now we will have to run into each other on a street corner or meet in the doctor's office, said Helen.

— Mary-Adeline I would like to wish you good luck with your recital. Hope it goes well for you tonight, Harold said to her.

They were interested, and they asked her about the recital that he had referred to that she was to perform that evening. She provided information as to where she was performing, and said a little something about what the program was that she was to present.

— Then I believe that that concert hall is a new building, is it not? asked Karol.

— It is state of the art, yes, said Mary-Adeline.

Dump trucks were driving by.

— It is too bad this, she said to say goodbye to them. She headed off.

They went on.

— She's that violinist of that music you gave to me, and with that field of a garden, said Helen.

— She is. It was nice of her to come out, he said.

— I wish I hadn't, she said.

They arrived at Helen's house.

— I knew I shouldn't have come.

— Mother, you were going to no matter what.

— I was not. I wasn't. I only let you talk me into it. I shouldn't have gone. I shouldn't have let you talk me into it.

She went into her house.

— I hope she is not going to become difficult in her old age, Karol said to him.

— That is to be hoped for.

They were home.

— Few appreciate change even when it's for the better, she said to him.

— Or that's all we want.

— I understand why. Change bothers me as well, or I suppose you would think I'm not like everyone else? she asked.

He would have preferred not to know.

— Are you free for lunch today? I'll be working on other preparations. I might want some of your advice. We could have lunch together.

— I won't have time. Then you don't need my advice, Karol.

— All right, never mind.

They got into their cars to go to work.

II

At the top floor he got out of the elevator. He climbed up the last flight of stairs. He unlocked the door. He returned the key to its hiding spot. He stepped outside. Rain was pouring down.

He walked out onto the flat roof into the rain. He went on across the roof to where his work colleague and friend was standing under an umbrella. She held her umbrella up for him. He ducked to get under it.

— You got wet, she said to him.

— Not as much as I deserve to.

Thirty stories below on the sidewalks and at the crosswalks moving along were umbrellas.

— I must thank you for having made off with the roof key Friday, as I might have come here and spent the afternoon lost in thought, as I am now, I'm nearly lost in thought. You can imagine why? You can't. I can't myself really.

He took from her the umbrella to hold, so that she might rest her arm. She smiled at him.

— Now why's that?

— You'd be right to think something's troubling me. Something is troubling me. This morning I witnessed the demolition of our town church. A few months ago I had heard about it being torn down. At the time I didn't do anything to find out what was going on. I knew there were those unhappy about it. I might have been more curious. Then what was done to tear it down and nothing to save the building, which should or might remind us, you and me, of what never gets accomplished and we are of those who haven't managed to do the job expected of us. Then last night, as I was contemplating matters my conscience revealed to me what I would not want to think about.

— It does not sound like you can do much about that.

— So you and I know the names of more living things than for any practical purpose, but what are we accomplishing from our hard work if anything?

She took a hold of the umbrella. They held onto it together.

— But what motivates us when we suspect the universe is expanding out into nothingness and later maybe shrinking and on its way into turning into a black hole that it is to disappear into? Expanding and shrinking again and again. How long can that go on for, and what difference does it make if that is all there is to be hoped for from the entire failing universe?

He stepped out from under the umbrella into the rain. There was rumbling of thunder in the distance.

— You're suggesting that you'd like to give up on your convictions maybe? she asked.

— That's an idea. I shall do that.

— You want to give up on your strongly held convictions?

— Or the opposite has to be true.

— You're not convinced?

— Neither one way or another.

— What I've always thought, in your case, Harold, is that what you have to do is express yourself with real passion. You maybe need to and you could scream. You should scream if you want to. Scream a little, if you'd like to. You might want to.

— But Isa, there's fate that makes no difference as to what allows us to be more or less satisfied or unsatisfied in any given moment.

— You ought to scream, it would help and do you some good. You have to let it go once in a while.

Then for him as his friend, to demonstrate how much conviction she as a woman had, in comparison to how little he would have been willing to express himself, as a faint-hearted man—she screamed. She shrieked from a place inside one's self that was not threatening, but somewhat frightening. The piercing sound was unsettling. She screamed hysterically and wildly laughed without the slightest inhibition.

— What are you doing? he asked.

— Who will hear us?

From her guts she moaned unintelligibly.

— Someone might hear you, he whispered.

The Unorthodox Ox

— I scream, you whisper, 'Be careful.' We are not alone up here? We are alone. What is the problem? It's pouring down. No one will hear us. You shouldn't worry about what I might think about you or maybe you should.

She brought her umbrella down and she pointed the end at him, and she poked him with it in the soft spot of his stomach.

— Or squeal, she screamed.

He stepped back and moved off from her. She poked him in the small of his back and he squealed.

— Where are you going? You won't get far.

She went after him as he walked off and she was shouting at him for how he didn't know how to express himself with any passion.

— Let's hear a peep out of you, she screeched.

— Stop that.

— I will not until I hear you scream bloody murder.

He got up onto a ledge so that she would maybe stop poking him.

— Go ahead, push me over the edge. Toss me over.

— Look at you. You are tempting fate? How clever is that? You shouldn't. Get down from there.

She poked him again. He got down. She held the umbrella up. He got under it. They wiped the rainwater off themselves.

— What I'd like to confess to if I knew what it was, he said.

— Harmlessness.

— If that were an excuse I'd confess to that, yes.

— You trust me to confess to being harmless?

— I do.

— Which is why I trust you as well.

— Don't. Because who can we trust?

They looked out into the rain. Lightening flashed over them.

They began discussing the business of their work.

— The *Rhino Beetle Report,* who would have thought that a Rhino Beetle could be endangered? That such a fecund bug could come under threat?

She sighed.

— No place for them to burrow, nowhere to run and hide.

— Apparently not.

— Nowhere to go.

— Is that why?

— Or there is something we don't understand, if we knew what it was. What is it that we do not understand?

Isa Martin de Aguilera was a person for whom he would have done anything for had she been interested, and had he himself been able.

Far down below them there were office workers going inside the office buildings to remain even if the sun were to come out.

Under her umbrella they crossed the roof.

— Then I might tell you that my wife has me participating in the *Frogwatch Program*. We are supposed to be going out together to participate in the evenings and in the mornings. I'm taking my work home with me more than I'd like to or should.

— You shouldn't do that.

— I knew you'd feel for me.

— Yes.

— I am to be pitied.

— You are.

— Am I not? You pity me.

— If you ask me to.

— Because I can't stand self-pity. I appreciate your sympathy.

— You do.

— I do.

— Then enjoy the *Species Assessment Report*, she laughed.

— You shouldn't say that.

— I know, but enjoy yourself regardless.

They went to their offices.

§

He knew what the *Species Assessment Report* was to report, what the purpose was, what the presentation was going look like, what the factual and qualified information had to reveal and deal with.

The charts, graphs, and the written descriptions detailed approximately the time, place, and the speed of inevitable change. There were one hundred and fifteen species endangered, eighty-two threatened, twenty-eight extirpated, there were listings of extinctions:

The Unorthodox Ox

recent extinctions, upcoming ones and a list of previous historical disappearances.

There were in appendixes pictures and hand-drawn illustrations. Before he was to begin his analysis, he leafed through them. He admired the pictures of a number of varieties of dead ducks.

They were truly and masterfully rendered illustrations and there was one picture, with its accompanying rendering of the extinct Great Auk, it caught his eye.

The pictures and anatomical illustrations, he spent time on them, examining them nostalgically.

Then the usual mistakes in the report he found as he worked through the data. He discovered the common sort of discrepancies and inequalities in the math of the calculations. The errors he knew to fault to inattentiveness on the part of those responsible for them. So it was when he was going through, around, and back and over several related errors that he discovered a sequence of reoccurring mistakes that kept coming up. His feet were beginning to swell from slowing circulation. He untied his laces and took his shoes off.

And coming across a particular problem, he was working back through it as required and he ended up at several dead-ends, and then he found what he was looking for, the original and glaring mistake.

So he wrote suggestions for the corrections that would be revised again and would come back to him again, and he would find new mistakes in the corrections and he would send them back again and so on.

He eased his feet back into his shoes. He went to speak with his assistant and to give her the report. She was to return it to those who were going to make the revisions.

Then for the problems in the report that the contributors to it had been unable to resolve, his assistant reminded him that the usual mistakes always had to be made. He stomped a foot to make sure his shoe was on.

— That's true and if it wasn't always the case? That would be encouraging. But what is there to do to inspire others to get them to be conscientious and mindful of what they are supposed to do? Then why should we have to do that? Because here we are determining prospects for life on the planet, if there are any, if we can live without them and maybe not. How we can live without them? And it's not just for human life, not just our miserable human lives, for all of life! For all our fellow creatures who can't count on us for their survival, not with our mutual extinction on the horizon. So we are aware that what we're trying to do is relevant and relatively important. Then is it not interesting to know that what we are doing matters in explaining to what degree the world is doomed and how, why, and when it will happen? It should make a difference to be on the right track, after the right solutions. It should matter more than we know or suspect. It should. Should it not?

He pointed at a stuffed frog on her desk. There were on the other desks in the surrounding office cubicles stuffed frogs sitting upright.

— Then those stuffed animals! Christ Almighty! I gave my approval for that! I thought, why not? I gave the go ahead, not for a good reason, only because, why not? It was not a good idea. It was a bad idea. Then perhaps my standing is not what it was or should be as a result of such a decision to have stuffed frogs made to order. Does such a decision compromise my ability to command respect? Am I no longer to be taken seriously as an authority? Is that what is happening? Is that the situation that I have found myself in? So I have lost my credibility. What if that is what is happening? If my credibility is shot? If it is buggered? If I have become another headless figurehead on a rudderless boat.

His assistant humoured him as necessary.

— I hope that's not the case. Then I'm having trouble breathing. I am short of breath. I am overwhelmed. I'm going to go out, and you can tell anyone who asks for me. Tell them that I don't want to have to be the one to tell anyone anything at the moment, right now. I don't even know when I will be or if I will be able to even.

— I shall return the chapters to everyone, she assured him.

— Make that a priority and priorities are useful. When in doubt always have a few good priorities. There's nothing to worry about if we have at least one available priority that's as important and urgent as ever at our disposal.

He laughed to dissimulate his own and maybe also her preoccupation.

— What if I've lost track of what the priorities are? Then respect has to do with choosing the right priorities. There's a connection

The Unorthodox Ox

between the two, a close connection, one in the same, almost is what they are. Have I lost track of what our priorities are? I will be challenged for that if I have. I will be of no use to anyone, to those in need of assistance and in need of the right priority that I'm responsible for providing. I'd be buggered. I would be.

He walked away into the maze of office cubicles, away from the fixed gaze of many hundreds of stuffed frogs sitting out on all the desks, and they were looking after him from under half-closed eyes and seemingly they might have appeared to be following him relentlessly as he was scurrying off.

He went down in the elevator and out the building and into a gusting wind that had come up that was blowing around the skyscrapers. Rain was sheering down. He was soon wet again.

He was walking for a time and before long, enough time had passed for his absence to be appreciated by those who would have asked for him. He kept on going nevertheless, and it might not have mattered where he was going until he arrived at the entrance of a public biosphere, and it would not have made a difference if he had ventured inside the open biosphere or stayed out in the rain. He entered the indoor rainforest to get out of the rain.

The habitat, it was a model for urbanites, who were interested to learn about unfamiliar vegetation that grew in such a tropical habitat, as it would have in a possible authentic environment, but it was not authentic and was conceptual, more than it was true to nature.

There were visitors walking around and strolling on wood chip paths that went around, under, and through bushes and beneath the taller trees of the model rainforest.

Wild birds were calling out in a recording. There was a heaviness in the air, it was soothing to inhale the warm thickness of its moistness.

He went headlong into the sanctum of the place.

He got on to a main thoroughfare that circled in a circumference and spiralled up in a gentle incline around the outer edges up to a domed glass ceiling and up to an observation platform near the dome's top where there was a close-up view of the upper canopy and a bird's eye view of the jungle below. It was a rest spot. Then lying on the floor of the observation deck was an old man, sleeping, despite the recorded shrieking of Keel-billed Toucans and Violaceous Trogons that in the wild would have been positioned in a Cecropia tree.

He stopped to take a breather. He looked out into the vegetation.

People were coming and leaving the platform. They stopped and commented on the greenness of the forest, on the size of the tropical leaves, and to admire the fanciful naturalness of it. They were to look at the sleeping homeless man. Some voiced their displeasure at the sight of the man's sorry state. He was old, poorly dressed, but likely not a burden to anyone but himself. He would have been dreaming of better days, otherwise would not have been sleeping at all. The sound of an angry Toucan woke the man up. He asked out loud why he was awake and he lay down to go back to sleep. Sprinklers came on. The mist in the air thickened. The recorded birds were quiet.

Walking on his way back to his office a car driving through a puddle splashed him. Harold didn't mind.

He was returning earlier than he might have wanted. He had not eaten lunch as he had thought he wouldn't have that morning.

His assistant looked at him with concern because of his appearance, but she was not to mention that anything was amiss.

A revised *Species Assessment Report* she informed him was already ready for him to look over, what were the first of the initial preliminary corrections had been addressed. He had to have been gone longer than he thought. He took the revised report from her.

In his office he changed into a different pair of clothes that he had on hand for such occasions, though no other similar occasion had occurred before.

He began to review the corrections and before long he came to a conclusion and he decided that he would have been better off to restrict his involvement for what he would have had to have done to look after what were the still uncorrected errors. So he called into his office the contributors, one by one, regarding each man and woman's corresponding contribution. Then for what were those individual sessions, he asked, what was the reason for him and each contributor to be discussing matters, and then to begin with he pointed out what his reason was and then after saying more about what he addressed generally he pointed out specifically that it was advisable for all those concerned to cooperate more and to consider the difficulties they were causing one another, and he suggested how it was important that each of them figure out who was doing what and that they should make more of an effort to make sure that what had to correspond accordingly would do so. His suggestions appeared to have made some difference.

He in return listened to proposals and to complaints that he had heard many times before.

There was a measure of compromise arrived at.

But there was then one statistician for whom he had to address problems that were a part of formulas in a series of equations that had gone awry in solving adjacent problems that ought to have led through a series of similar equations and so arrive at a series of solutions, but had failed to do so.

The objecting statistician, the man was an apologist, and there in his office the man was smiling apologetically for no reason, and it was not reasonable that statistically the statistician was defending an assumption that was that the uncorrected mistakes were due to the data itself.

— I don't see that. The data is fine. No, nothing is wrong with the data, he said to the man.

The statistician was not as apologetic as he appeared, and he presented the idea that if there was more margin for error on either side of what did not maybe add up that the results would not be the same and different.

— Not at all. We left plenty of room for error. There is more than enough room for error. That is the last thing that is needed is more room for error.

He was looking at an ill-proportioned oval shaped face, asymmetrical, with a narrow round opening for a mouth, one zero inside another. Stubs of teeth were being held in place by receding gums. He was insincerely smiling and discharging a stench into the air from the decay of poor oral hygiene.

— No, it is necessary to understand the information. The data is fine. No one would imagine that the facts we have are incorrect, not when we see what has already been proven. If there is anything we can be sure of it is that, and that there is no more room for error required.

Then he got to the point in explaining the point he was after making of having to almost define the elementary number theory, and he alluded to: integer factorization, quadratic reciprocity, the Chinese remainder theory, and Fibonacci numbers, and he was going to have to go further in his explanation, but he lost his patience. He could not restrain himself. He shouted out furiously.

— You must think that if an evolutionary process makes use of the advantage of non-compressibility of the primes to produce organisms, that we are also capable of proving the opposite? One and the opposite are both true? In the same gasping breath? Is that possible, do you think? Is that idea of interest to us? Is that the kind of margin for error that we can tolerate and live with?! Is it? Is that the idea? Jesus Christ Almighty!

The argument was coming to a conclusion.

— Is this what we are getting at? You mongrel idiot! You rat-brained fool! You nitwit! It isn't! No, it isn't! You mindless runt of a half-wit! What is wrong with you people?

— Well... er...

— What do I have to do? Insult you? And do you understand a word I've said? Then have I said something that stands the test? But what is it that stands the test? Then do you know your real name and who was responsible for giving it to you?

The statistician was apologizing.

— You want to excuse yourself? Did I ask for an excuse? Did I say, excuse yourself? Did I ask that? No, I don't want excuses. I will never ask for excuses. I am not here to listen to useless excuses! Not yours nor my own! Can we not spare ourselves from the excuses of our inexcusable failings?! Can we not do that at the very least?! Can we not do that much?! For once, just for once! For once in a day! Screw this pointless stupidity, the hell with it!

He ordered the man to get out of his sight and to remain there if he would.

§

Harold opened his office door. It was quiet on the outside. He observed the overall subdued hush. He looked out over the open office space. He let out an inaudible triumphant snort, but he was defeated.

He went back into his office.

For the afternoon he went over overdue personnel changes that he had to make. He made decisions on the renewing and the cancelling of contracts. He figured out what positions to eliminate permanently and temporarily. He worked out the scheduled time frame for doing so.

Then later he asked for the studies on the Piping Plovers for them to be brought to him, the "first studies" from when the *Protection Designation* had been awarded. Those documents he read over and he confirmed how there had been fewer conflicts of interest at one time and fewer obstacles. He read about what had once been accomplished before and he made his comparisons to what were to be the newest requirements, and he thought about what the constraints were. He figured out how to budget money and how to coordinate the work that was to be done. And he devised optional plans in case his suggestions were refused or labelled as being unfeasible, and to a degree of satisfaction he came up with alternatives based on variations of his plans to restore the Piping Plover's nesting grounds.

No one had interrupted him throughout the afternoon. Not even a call had come in for him.

Then it was in the early evening when he was feeling almost a little lonely in his office. Isa Martin de Aguilera stopped by to speak with him.

— I was told I should not disturb your highness.

— I lost it.

— Your aplomb?

— I overstated my case.

— What could have happened to your unshakable aplomb?

— I've been under some stress as I mentioned.

— You took to heart what I said to you this morning?

— You're to blame, maybe, yes.

— I helped you to say what has to be said more forcefully sometimes.

— I couldn't help myself.

— There was a lunatic on the loose. I could hear you from my office howling away.

— It won't happen again.
— It was an impressive performance.
— It was shameful, I know.
— It was a magnificent performance. I never would have thought you had it in you.
— I am feeling sheepish about it.
— You shouldn't.
— But he is a problem that man, a symptom of systemic social rot.
— I congratulate you.
Then she saw what he was working on.
— So I heard about the Plovers. Were you going to let me know?
— What can I say?
— Who would do such a thing, destroy a nesting ground, and why?
— Malcontents and the disaffected, I don't know and I don't know why. Maybe it was because of the incomprehensible Latin and French on the signs. We know how we get when we don't understand what we are being told or saying. We will become violent, destructive, abusive, and foolish. I don't know why. Then ask why the *Frogwatch Program* will bring us down. It will be our undoing I promise you.
— Yes, that English intern is making an impression in distributing your stuffed mascots.
— The English like to make impressions. They are a damnable group of people.
— But you know how it is to want to make an impression. You do.
— Yes.
— The Latin signs made a bad impression?
— Likely as anything.
— We don't know how to impress each other like we should then.
— No.
— But you and I impress each other of course.
— We do.
— Then maybe some day when I get around to writing my memoirs I will say something about how we as colleagues impressed

one another. I'm going to write my memoirs one day, I think.

— I've always known you would, Isa.

— I'll include you: the man with whom I worked.

— Thank you, I would be honoured to be in your memoirs.

— I will honour you.

— Already I am flattered.

— Then how would you like to be portrayed?

— Not well, I imagine.

— I could portray you as a good-hearted man, fair-minded, never unkind to anyone.

— It would be kind of you to say so, even if you don't mean it.

— How would you like to be portrayed? I might ask for your help in my portrayal of you. You even could be interested to write your own introduction. You might pass along some of the information I'll need. We'll write it together, starting from? From the beginning, I imagine. Then I'd start out by saying: 'How it was rewarding to have worked side by side with such an upstanding individual, with a man of such foresight. It was a pleasure.'

— Don't we have enough to write as it is?

— 'My close friend, my dear friend, he had to say that everything was always worse than it was. He would say that whenever he had the chance. He had the ability to look into the blackest hole inside the night.'

— It would be accurate to say that.

— 'I suspect he had reason to. And I think I understood why so much was troubling for him. I understood that as his close confidant. Then in part it was because of his dark mysterious past.' But what don't I know about your past background that I might include that I don't know much about? What don't I know or have ignored about what you like to grouse about constantly? About what has always been as bad as it could have been. You can think of something.

— I can.

— The worse the better, play along with me, come on.

— All right, I can, O.K., yes, you might mention how I had crawled out of the gutter, though that is not an excuse for anything.

— I had forgotten that. It had to have been difficult for you to have found yourself in such an unfavourable environment.

— Yes, I was lucky to have survived and it was a matter of life and death at times.

— Yet here you are to tell me all about it.

— You might mention that I was guided by an invisible hand that I've never seen. How's that?

— 'He hadn't seen it. It was invisible as air,' she smiled at him.

— But eventually I was tired of looking for what was guiding me that was invisible to the naked eye and I concluded I can't keep trying to do that. It makes no sense.

— Don't be irreverent.

— No, irrelevant.

— You do not need to worry about what my perspective will be then.

— I should hope not.

— I'd like you to be impressed.

— I can still be impressed.

— 'He only screamed once and when he did, he whispered, "Forgive me, for making too much noise." What a cowardly and craven man he was at times and morally suspect as well I thought.'

— You can forgive me. Someone forgives me. I thank you for that.

— You're welcome.

They were to share other thoughtful words with each other, and they were ready to leave for the day.

— Then Isa, next week, I'm going away on holiday. I should get away for a bit. It's not good for me to be ill-treating people. I'll be going up north for the week.

— You're going on your honeymoon after all?

— After a fashion.

— So I'll be working away here. What would you do without me?

— I'd be friendless without you.

— You would be.

They were going down to the basement garage.

— Then you know what I'll be doing this evening? I'll be standing in a swamp with my wife and monitoring frogs, for God's sake.

— It won't be as bad as all that.

— Worse.

— Always worse, 'he always said.'

The Unorthodox Ox

They were leaving.

In the parking booth window there was sitting a stuffed frog, and while he was paying for his parking he asked the attendant about it. The man picked it up, and by way of demonstration he squeezed it. The frog croaked.

In the rear-view mirror when he was driving off he saw that the attendant was holding the toy up and he was examining it with an expression of disinterested detachment.

§

That other previous night after Mary-Adeline had privately played for him, afterwards, she had made a present to him of a recording of a performance of Ysaye violin sonatas; it was her first recorded performance, from her early years when her youthful perfected virtuosity still must have amazed her. Then in the morning when he had been driving into work he had listened to the recording and so he was listening to it for a second time as he was going home, and he added to his understanding and appreciation for what was Mary-Adeline MacSweeney's unfathomable expressiveness. Then maybe it occurred to him how remarkable it is that music is like a hymn to all the near deafening silence there is and it is like a calling to live without fearing death and to be at peace for that reason if for no other.

He drove out of the city. He was driving in the country and he was unmindful of everything as he was going and was putting everything that was in his mind consciously and unconsciously into its designated place.

How he would have liked to have gone to her recital that evening. But he had known that he couldn't have got away with it and that that would have been pressing his luck.

He came into the town. He pulled up to where the church had been.

Spread out over the empty vacant lot was a fresh layer of black dirt with grass seed sprinkled over it. There was a billboard advertising the demolition services that had done the job. Then there was the minister, he was sitting on the bench, looking out before himself forlorn.

He got out of his car to speak with him.
— George, how are you?
— How am I? I'm all right, thank you for asking, kind of you to ask, he almost whispered.
— Is there anything I can do for you?

If only there could have been something. He asked again if there might be anything, and he made an offer.

— I could give you a ride somewhere?
— No, I am not ready to go home.
— Neither am I. Then could I invite you for a drink?
— I could use one.
— You look like you could.
— I could do with a drink.
— Maybe it'll help to have a drink? Cheer you up.
— I don't know if it will.
— It's on me.

Then attempting to lessen the minister's sense of devastation as they were going along would not have succeeded. Neither would a drink really.

— Is there anywhere in particular where you want to go?
— Anywhere sounds fine.

They entered *Nowhere Inn Particular* (sic), and when the minister stepped in through the barroom door, up from their drinks all eyes in the place turned in his direction.

Customers, many who were regulars, they rose to their feet spontaneously. They applauded him. They called out his name. A dedication for his loss was asked for. The house publican offered to say a few words, he was also the proprietor of the bar and he professed humorously how he would be incensed if his business was destroyed by those who subscribed to abstinence. There was laughter. Someone who was everyone's friend bought a round for the house.

The pub, as the namesake suggested perhaps, was like such other places that provided escape for those who have few choices other than to spend years on stools or in chairs with drinks before themselves to get through the lonely days and long dark nights.

There were the usual and friendly groups of friends shouting and laughing over shared agreements and disagreements.

The Unorthodox Ox

They sat down at a table. They received their free drinks.

So at the table next to them there was a man who was relating a cautionary tale to his assembled friends.

— What is going to happen one day. Now listen. Hear me out. Heed my warning. You'll meet up with an enemy who's after revenge. You get home some time later. You've had a few drinks. You try to take your coat off. You can't get it off, because there's a knife stuck in your back. You didn't know you had been stabbed in the back. My friends, that is what innocence is, that is what being naïve is all about.

A friend clapped his hands approving.

— It can happen.

— I am worried about that, a woman at another table said.

— Then they're going to knock our houses down while we're sleeping. We'll wake up and have nothing, absolutely nothing, another said.

— After our insurance runs out. You can imagine.

— I wouldn't get insurance for that reason.

— There is no such thing as insurance, who are we kidding?

— No insurance?

— You're wrong, sir, another man nearby said, there is insurance. As a life insurance salesman I can tell you there is and I'll sell you some.

— Not on my life, you won't. Then he says to us we can buy it from him. How much?

— If you have money, but if you don't? What insurance is there if you haven't any money? If you're broke and you haven't got a cent to your name. Who is going to give you insurance if you can't pay an arm and a leg for it?

— But we have different policies to fit everyone's needs.

— You're a chancer. Do I look like I'm a betting man? Get away with you.

The discussions were to go on and other discussions would go on, on other evenings, while never coming to terms with their rightful grievances.

— These are good people. They are my kind of people, the folks of my flock. Thank you for inviting me, Harold. I feel a little better.

— I didn't want to leave you sitting there. I needed a drink myself.

— But I am crestfallen. I could cry into my drink. Then this morning, when Trudi left, she was as angry with me as I have ever seen her. She said she shouldn't have anything to do with me. She told me I was a cad. But I know she's too kind to be angry at me for long. I hope tomorrow she'll ask me to apologize for whatever it is that I've always done wrong. What if she doesn't? And I've never deserved her kindness. I didn't. She was decided. I was undecided, which shouldn't have been a problem. It was. It was a problem. Then I was thinking about when I first got to know her. I used to see her go by out in front of my house in the mornings and during the day. I'd be in my office working. I never got much work done afterwards. I'd go out to water the grass. She would be on her way going somewhere. I watered my lawn a lot at that time. I guess I thought if she saw me with a hose in my hand, you know what I mean. And I've a lot to reproach myself for. I never took my own advice. I knew what I had to do. So I've heard things from her students who had kind things to say about her.

They drank for a while without speaking. They listened to the conversations around them. They started in on another round and another round and another.

He brought up other recollections that he had. He waxed on about them. His failing hopes were common. But there would have been no telling him that what he was saying was the same as what most hoped for and never achieved. Harold was listening to him and was thinking maybe that it was going to be no different for himself one day. He would be a solitary figure, disconsolate, without faith, powerless, questionably loved, and what he would have to say for himself would be nothing more than what it was in actual fact.

— Another drink or two? asked George.

Harold should have already left by then. He was drunk.

— Harold, let me confess if I can, and I don't usually confess unless I've no choice, not even to the Almighty Himself. All right, I'd like to confess to having a drinking problem. Although that's not to say I haven't always enjoyed it. Then it's a vice that I've had since the first drink I took. I was predisposed. So I've kept it hidden from those I was close to, and I had to stay home to indulge by myself in order to escape too much public awareness. But I'd have

The Unorthodox Ox

preferred not to have had to keep it a secret, and I'd have been like these people here having a good time.

Which was as much as the minister was able to honestly confess to at that moment, but there had to have been more to it.

Then he had had more than he ever would have, and thinking it couldn't have been so much he had another drink that later he would have forgotten about, but he knew he had to stand up if he could and go home.

— I have to go home, George. I must go now.

— I don't have a home. My house of worship has been destroyed.

— I'm sorry. I wish I had known more about it. I wish I had. But the hell with it. It's not important what we believe or want, only what we do, what we actually do.

— No, it's important what we believe, too.

— It doesn't matter what anyone believes, not in the least. It doesn't matter.

— It's important what we believe. It is.

— You don't believe that. Give it a rest old man.

— I wonder if I don't?

— It's talking for the sake of it. You must know that even if you don't want to admit it, even if you don't want to believe it.

— Hard to say?

— It's always hard to say. No, it's not hard to say.

— I think it is.

— What?

They slapped each other on the back. The minister argued for him to have another.

— I must go.

— Your wife is expecting you?

— I could give you a ride home?

— No, that's all right, I am going to make a night of it. I am feeling a little better.

— What did I say?

— I think you said. I don't know.

— I'm going.

— You were leaving?

They patted each other on their backs.

§

On his hands and knees he was in the front yard momentarily almost unable to move. He was ill again. The second effort was not as difficult, but still a chore. He caught his breath. He wiped his nose and tears from his eyes. He cleared his throat of obstructions, spate them out. He gathered up his resources and crawled a ways. He fell onto his stomach. Again he was almost helpless. He flopped about to roll over onto his back. His eyes were open, he closed them and rubbed them and opened them. He was looking up at the moon and he was surprised by the white moonlight. Then he called out into the moonlit night the name of the Greek moon Goddess.

— Selene, you are putting me in a bad light. And it is not a hidden secret in the stars that I'm completely pissed out of my mind.

Then he was speaking out against Prometheus, whose liver he stated was in a similar state to his own. And there were the names of other Gods against whom he railed by their Greek or Roman names for his drunken amusement.

— Dionysus, Bacchus, and Silenus, who remembers you now at this point in time? But I curse you and all your deceased followers. And Christians, you sanctimonious self-righteous idolaters. Who is supposed to love you? Who loves you? Does God love you with all his infinite wisdom? You believe that?! You have no other choice but to believe that? You fools! So no, I will not drink your wine, because too much of it is hard to handle and it makes a man ill. Then you pie-faced Muslims with your lack of humour. Why don't you drink more? It might help you, you, you lover of camels.

He was making a racket and screaming once again that day, yelling at the top of his lungs without knowing that that was what he was doing.

Karol came out of the house. She asked him what was going on. What he was doing.

— You're asking me? What are you asking me? I don't know. Who knows? I've no clear idea. But I guess I'm not feeling too well. I am suffering from a sickness of the heart and I've a sick heart inside of me. I have a sore that is a hole that is my dead and rotting heart. But Karol, how are you tonight? How are things going for you this fine night? For you, on this night of all nights.

The Unorthodox Ox

— You've been drinking.

— I'll have to clean that mess up.

— You're hopelessly drunk. Aren't you?

— I didn't eat much today, nothing really, but there was something in me. Is that bile? Does that look like bile to you? Tell me if it is. Or have I thrown up my gangrenous heart? I have puked up my rotting and gangrenous heart.

— Why are you drunk?

— But how was your evening? You didn't go anywhere? I was hoping you would have gone out and wouldn't have been up waiting for me. That's why I've come home so late and because I had a little to drink.

— How were you able to drive?

— You might ask me how I was able to drive? Ask me how I was able to drive. Go ahead, ask me that. Stand there and ask me what you are asking me.

— Get up.

— Yes, I don't want to stay here. I would like to get up and go inside. Do you think the neighbours are home, do you think? What would they be doing in their house at this time of night? Are they sleeping? They're a lazy bunch of people, useless lazy bastards. You'll have to help me up. I am feeling lazy myself. Then I was with George, so he was beside himself from disbelief and unbelievable grief and for a man of faith to be beside himself from disbelief is a terrible sight. It is really terrible.

— Get up.

— I couldn't find words to say what I wanted to say to him. So do you think we could have made a case to save his godforsaken church? Do such cases exist in reality as we know it?

— Get up Harold.

— But no, maybe it's better to do nothing than to find out afterwards that there was nothing we could have done. I believe that? And you know, today, I read the *Species Assessment Report*, and so you and others ought to be aware of the fact that it's getting indisputable how the natural world is becoming unnatural, and so I wasn't surprised how I figured out what was what, and when doing so I realized as I was checking over old extinctions that I'll never have the opportunity to see a number of long gone dead ducks, neither will you, for that matter. Then I'd have liked to have seen a Labrador duck or a Great Auk. And it will be worse when we see the ones gone that we have seen in our lifetime. That will be one day to forget or never forget.

She helped him to his feet.

— I have soiled my trousers and shirt and let me take them off. Then it's already been reported by the retired school teacher that I was outside at night without my clothes on. So this would confirm that report, which is what is always needed, further proof of acts of confirmation. I have always liked that a lot. What is undeniable proof of acts of confirmation.

He pulled away from her. He tore off his shirt and he threw it over his own and the neighbour's fence. He dropped his trousers. She told him to pull them up. He refused or was unable to. She dragged him along and got him up the front steps. He was waddling with his pants down around his ankles.

— I would have liked to have seen a Labrador Duck. But in 1875 it was over for them, that was the year the Labrador Duck disappeared off the face of the earth, but fortunately we as the descendants of those alive at the time aren't responsible, and it may have been an act of nature more than man. Though that wasn't the case in 1844 for the Great Auk. That was caused as a result of the actions of our ancestors. The Great Auk couldn't fly. They weren't flying birds. And on Funk Island, the inhabitants of Funk Island, I mean the visitors to Funk Island (no one inhabited the place, it smelled of shit), and whoever those insensitive cocksuckers were they robbed the Great Auk's nests of eggs and took them home to fry them for breakfast. So our ancestors drove the Great Auk into extinction by scrambling their eggs for breakfast. But you don't believe me. You think I have the wrong dates? Those are the dates. And if you want you can ask me the dates of any extinct animal you can think of. I'll tell you. I will tell you the year of their extinction, the exact year. Because I am paid to know it and it interests me to keep track of dates of extinction. But you doubt me?

— Do I?

They went inside.

— You should doubt me, but you should do so for a reason instead of whenever you get the chance for no reason, as you always

The Unorthodox Ox

do. God Karol, I have to wonder if you hate me more than anyone who has ever lived and if I hate you more than anyone who has ever lived. Do we hate each other more than anyone who has ever lived? Is that the problem?

— I don't always have a reason?

— It's been a while since I've spoken out of turn. When was the last time I said something out of turn? Can we remember exactly when that was? Can we remember that?

— I have a reason now.

— But this, what is this? What depravity is this before me?

In the front room, he was staggering unsteadily, and he was looking down at design plans that were laid out on the floor, and there were photographs of caged men and women incarcerated; they were looking out from behind bars or through little windows with expressions on their faces of despair and crushing hopelessness.

— You were working on floor plans. I'm taking you away from what you were doing. I could have stayed in the yard.

She set about gathering up the papers and photographs in case he might have stumbled and tromped on them.

— Pull up your pants you ass-hole.

He struggled in attempting to do so, he succeeded.

— I should have come back later. Had I known you were at work I'd have come back much later, tomorrow even.

— So Harold, Wednesday I leave, Wednesday I'm leaving, she said.

— Wednesday? You're leaving? Wednesday? For good? Then that's sooner than you thought. I'll miss you. And I'll get drunk while you are away. Oh, I feel sorry for you and for us. You have no idea how sorry I feel for us. I feel sorry for you especially and for myself.

— I was not expecting you to be drunk.

— Yet I wanted to tell you that's what I had in mind. You know now and it doesn't matter.

— Then there's something for you to consider, even if you are drunk out of your mind. I have another reason to be angry at you.

He repeated several times that she was leaving.

— Wednesday? You're leaving. Wednesday?

— Look at this. Read it.

— You're leaving?

— That is what I said!
— Wednesday?
She handed him what she wanted him to read.
— Let this sober you up.
— This coming Wednesday.
— I said. Read what it says.
— What did you say?
— You are not going to make me repeat myself. I am not going to repeat myself another time! Read it!

She said something else that he couldn't listen to as he was doing as she had asked.

— Karol, would it be possible for you to give me one moment's peace, one moment?! Because how am I supposed to concentrate with you barking in my ear like a wild rabid hyaena. Quiet!
— Yes, I can be quiet. Can you?
— No. I will never be quiet.

He said something that was incomprehensible that he himself had not understood, but he understood what she had given him to read. He understood it perfectly and altogether well enough.

— It's a lot of money, the price we have to pay for the sins of others and our own, he said.
— There has to be a mistake, she trumpeted.
— Perhaps it's possible, I should hope so. I shall look it over.
— We'll make a counterclaim, she demanded shrilly.

There was the book value, the repair and the replacement costs itemized.

— I see the purchase cost and that the figures are exorbitant. It looks like nothing is underestimated. No one underestimates anything when after money. They are looking to upgrade the facilities likely, and they'll take advantage of us to do so. We're the suckers. Of course, the Councillor is the kind of unscrupulous weasel who knows how to take advantage of situations. He must believe we will accept this. It can't be helped. However, we should think it can be, I think. Although this is the kind of thing that happens when one's luck runs out. Then this is a wake up call. No, we shouldn't have to pay this. And I think we shouldn't be taken advantage of, and I will not allow you nor myself to be fleeced while alive. We can pay the right amount, there can't be anything wrong with that, and there

The Unorthodox Ox

is no denying that there's anything wrong with that. This is a wake up call. I'll speak with him and tell him there's been a mistake. So I have had to deal with these political grafters who don't know that everything is not for their benefit. Then maybe I'll speak with him now. I've a mind to. I'm in the mood. And the Councillor had to have known about this this morning when I spoke to him at the demolition. He said nothing, not a whisper. Why not? Yes, I'm going to go and talk with him right now because I might as well. Why not? I will tell him what is on my mind right now.

He headed towards the door, opened it, he walked out.

— But perhaps I ought to change my clothes first? No, I will change into my pyjamas when I return and sleep with my mind at ease.

He stepped back inside. He took a coat from a rack by the door to cover his naked torso.

— Harold, what do you think you are doing?

— Do not herald me, Karol. I am not your king. You are not my coronated queen. Although maybe you ought to come along. We'll go as a couple, the aggrieved party. Then if we had not got married none of this would have happened. We're the ones to blame really.

— Get in the house.

— So Elrod is going to bill us as taxpayers for demolishing the church and we're paying them to destroy everything. Then they are the rich destroyers of everything that we hold dear that people like us want to keep and that we have high regard for. But you and I have also been destructive people as well. And it's people like us who have no respect for anything either, not really, no, we don't. We have no respect, not even for ourselves. We are lacking in self-respect! I think.

He walked out into the street.

— You want to be ridiculous?

— That is all I have ever wanted. And go to bed. I don't want you to be awake when I return, he shouted as he walked away into the dark.

A light next-door came on. A window slammed.

Above where the church had been a night-hawk was flying. It was preying on poor homeless church mice.

§

He rang the doorbell and rang it again after the door opened.
— Could you stop ringing, would you please stop ringing the bell?
— Good evening Elrod. How are you this evening?
— Do you know what time it is? the Councillor asked him.
— I've woken you up. I was hoping you might still be up, and you are now. Might we have a word, as we did not finish this morning's conversation?

Then Councillor Elrod knew what it was for and about. He had his prepared defense. He had answers ready. So in the entrance on either side of it, the men argued their arguments.

The Councillor, first after listening to what was the opening gambit, responded.

— You have to understand that adjusters when they're determining accurately a settlement will account for what is covered and for what the liabilities are.
— In whose interest? asked Harold.
— You don't appreciate it not being in your interest understandably.
— In the interest of whom?! Whose interest?!
— Of the municipality. Please, not so loud.
— I'm thrilled to no end to have to pay more than my fair share or anyone's fair share to such an interest. I am not!
— My wife and children are asleep.
— That amount of money is prohibitive and is unreasonable and is unjustifiable.
— If you had looked the contract over for what the parties were liable for, you would have realized that the indemnity clause specified what the coverage covered, and you should have had additional coverage. It was unfortunate that you didn't consider what might be considered to be divine acts. That's always the safest route.

They challenged one another on what were legal points and for what was either right or wrong, but in the end, there was almost as much credibility afforded to one and the other, and they had to come to what was temporarily an unsatisfactory conclusion, which was that the last of it had not been heard of.

The Unorthodox Ox

— What else then? What else? I'll tell you what. I know for a fact, that for the church to be so conveniently levelled that there were no public consultations, no publicized notice went out that there were going to be open consultations. Then Elrod, explain to me, if you can, explain this, tell me, why were you the one to come to tell me that my mother had passed away?! Because who were you to tell me? You had no business to be bringing me such traumatic news! Someone who has a heart should have been the one to tell me that she was gone, someone who knows what compassion is.

— I believe I said that I had received information from a medical examiner, and that is why I told you. I said I was sorry to be the one to tell you at the time.

— Anyone would have known someone else had to bring me that news. I don't know you. And you're someone who doesn't know any better. Then the open graves! Miss MacSweeney's cat that you brought her! You don't know what you are doing. You're out of control. You're a loose canon firing at random. You're a failed overachiever!

From upstairs then there were voices and out onto a landing came a sleepy woman with young children at her side.

— Honey, is there a problem? she called down the stairs.

— You must leave now. It is late.

— I'd have come earlier, but I was consoling the pastor for your work.

— We can talk another time.

— That's your wife. She's asking what the problem is. Should we ask her what the problem is?

— It's O.K. Dear.

She said she hoped so and she and the children lumbered off.

— Those children are your offspring and you are their ancestor. Good God, don't we feel for them? Don't we feel for them? Then let us pity those who will follow us.

— You must leave now.

— Why not? But give me a reason.

— It's my house. It is late.

— Yes, I was worried when no one answered the door that I had come to the wrong address.

— We will talk another time.

— So you're really saying there is no room for compromise, and I would compromise if I were in your position. And that's why you need to listen to my opinion and I'll tell you that you don't know what it's like to be amongst those who can help his fellow man and you are not the kind of good-hearted man who knows what it is like to share in feelings of solidarity and feel compassion for others and to empathize with others. You don't know what it's like to be a kind and good human being.

— Oh, I am sorry, it is too bad you feel that way and I suppose it is unlikely that I can influence you into changing your mind, but you might think to change it, then think otherwise. You might. Then actually I do have some information to share with you of interest for you to be informed of. You haven't been notified yet. You were going to be. You see, recently, we finalized an allocation reassessment, federally, provincially, and at a municipal level. So there has been a reallocation of budgets and a reassigning of jurisdictional responsibilities to make better use of resources and revenues and enforcement authority. And the issue to do with your concern is for the protection areas that for their maintenance and policing are to be under municipal governance from now on. This will eliminate overlapping services and conflicts of interest that we were having and were unnecessarily complicated and were even becoming unlawful our legal advisers determined.

— Is that right?

— I've been apprised of the violation of the Piping Plover site. So we will see to its restoration and look after an investigation. I'll send the information to you.

— I'm glad to hear this.

— You will receive a report. Now please leave.

— I was about to. I thank you for your time.

— Another time would have been better.

He couldn't help expressing to Councillor Elrod, as he was walking off, that he was pleased something was going to be done for the Piping Plovers, and he related a few facts for what the bird's habitat needed and why it needed to be protected. He mentioned that no one would have reason to regret an increase in their population, especially given that there was a high risk of their extinction.

When he came to the end of the walkway the front yard light

The Unorthodox Ox

went off. He tripped on the curb in the dark.

— Where am I? he asked.

The last remaining lights that had been on in the houses were off. The townspeople were sleeping in their beds or were beside them down on their knees in the town where there was nowhere left for them to pray.

How to manage the kind of boundless man that was the Councillor is a challenge, and there are those men who march to the rhythm of their beat that they loudly drum. They cannot be stopped. The only hope is that they will stop themselves. They will not.

He was going by the church lot, and he looked to where the steeple would have risen and to where the light in the sky of the north star was shining, and he wished on it and one wish became several other wishes, hoping for the previous one, but all of them were indifferent to prospects of coming true.

Nothing happened for as long as he remained there. He headed on home. A night-hawk was calling behind him. A terrified mouse squeaked in the night.

She was awake.

— It might have helped if you had come along. Then I give that man credit for knowing how to play his clever game.

— You were not as convincing as you might have been then?

— I might have been if you had been there, Karol.

— You'll have to be more convincing.

— I should have punched him in the nose?

— I hope you didn't.

— I might have. I don't remember, he shook a fist in the air.

He cleaned himself up and got ready for bed, and he brushed his skin to maybe appease her.

— I feel weak all of the sudden, he said when flat on his back in bed.

— You are weak.

— I'm not so drunk now, and I can't imagine why I drank so much. I let myself go. I never do that. I shouldn't have. Because it's not comforting after a point. Not like it is for George for whom drinking is a comfort, as is his God. He has God and the bottle for comfort.

— You'll be sorry tomorrow, Harold.

— You'll make sure of that.

— You'll be sure of it yourself. I don't have to tell you that.

— But you did.

They were waiting to go to sleep.

— Then I went out to monitor the frogs without you this evening, she said.

— Did you?

— I noticed no difference.

— Oh well.

— Not that I could hear. So I got a lot done today. It was a productive day for me. Then I am starting to understand what the constraints are that we have to work under. They're limiting. I was looking over the design models as you noticed earlier. It seems like they are all more or less the same. There is not much room for creativity. Of course, there wouldn't be.

— Karol, believe me when I say I do not object, I don't, and I would not want to hinder you from making a contribution to the building of a facility as secure as any that has been built. And anyway, when we stop to think about it we know that we're all imprisoned. But what kind of prison is the one to be in? The one built for us or the one we build ourselves? One might be better than the other. But there is no escape from one or the other. Yes, I think that life as we know it is a prison and there is no escape from it except death.

— You should go to sleep.

— You don't want to know what my objections could be, even if I objected.

— I am not going to listen to them now.

— Listen to your heart. It is she in her wisdom who knows the truth about what she has to say. Follow her sound advice. That is what I would suggest. Take the advice of your heart to heart.

They were quiet for a moment. He was losing his will to remain attentive.

— You're not asleep yet, she accused him.

— You said I should be.

— I just want to tell you that tomorrow afternoon I'm going on an *Inside Justice Tour*, that is what they call it, to see what it's like on the inside. Then today I spoke to an architect who told me that

The Unorthodox Ox

he had spent a couple of days locked up to see what it is like, and he had found it helpful to spend time in the space to get a feel for it. He said to me that the experience altered his ideas. He had made design changes as a result, he said. I thought it was an interesting idea. So what if I were to spend a few days in jail? To see what it's like. I would have to ask for permission. Is it a crazy idea, isn't it?

— No harm in asking.

— You could visit me.

— I could.

— It is madness to even consider it.

— I think you should consider it. I think you should seriously consider spending some time in jail.

He was hardly listening to her as she was speaking about theories she had been working on for what it is like to live in a 198 by 289 cm cell for many years on end, and she had come up with an understanding, it was different to his way of thinking. In the middle of her explanation he fell asleep.

In the morning when out monitoring in the swamps and at home later and when they were getting ready to go to work, neither of them referred to his previous night's indulgence. But she did say as he was leaving that she hoped he would enjoy his day and not work too hard, and he shouldn't come home late, as he would need to get a good night's sleep, she admonished him.

He took care as he drove to work as he was unsure of his sobriety.

§

He called his assistant and for the intern, for the two of them to come along to his office.

He picked up the stuffed frog from under his desk lamp. He turned the light off. He got up from his desk. He walked around from behind it to welcome them when they arrived.

— Good morning, he said.

They answered cautiously in kind.

— I've asked for you to come for what could not be of less importance than if it was for none at all. I apologize for that. It is insignificant. I shouldn't bother. I'm obliged to. I apologize for it.

He inquired how they were. They were well, but would not have been in position to complain.

— Yesterday evening when I was paying for my parking I couldn't help but notice that there was a frog on display in the parking booth window, and the attendant in his booth, the uninformed man, he didn't know what it was for. Now the distribution has gone very well, I thank you for that, Miss Llewellyn. But you know, if we are to pass these frogs out to all and sundry, I think that our cause would be better served if recipients knew what they were for, which is why we provide information to those who receive them, otherwise, we're handing them out as if for no reason whatsoever and might not bother.

He stopped to let what he was saying sink in and to possibly amuse himself.

— I imagine he would have received a pamphlet with it, said Miss Llewellyn.

— Yet the man in his booth didn't know what it was for. He was being duplicitous? I don't know why such a person would do such a thing.

— He might not have read what he was given? she asked.

— I suppose we can't assume that anyone will read what we give them, you're right, that's a pertinent point, he said.

— Perhaps there was a different man in the booth who was given the frog at a different time and he could have taken the pamphlet home with him and left the frog behind, said his assistant.

— A different man in the booth at a different time and one taking the pamphlet home and leaving the frog behind could explain it. But I would think that it'd be more likely for someone to have taken the frog home then left the pamphlet behind, assuming he had one. Anyway, that's that problem solved. Then Ms. Llewellyn, I want to thank you for your work that in a short time has measured up. But isn't it a shame? That there is no way to get people to read what will inform them. There is nothing we can do. We can point them in the right direction, but that's it, and if it pleases whoever it is, they can remain ignorant until the day they die and rest easy knowing that for their entire lives they were absolute ignoramuses and they have inflicted untold harm without even realizing it.

She suggested that she could provide the attendant with another

The Unorthodox Ox

pamphlet, and she would do what she could to get him to read it and she might explain what she could to him directly, if that would help.

— There's probably no point, thank you very much, he said.

— I would be pleased to do what I could.

— Nothing else, that's it, thank you.

As asked of her the intern saw herself out the door.

— I was saying that that was of no importance. So she's a little cheeky that woman, he said.

— She is eager to please, said his assistant.

— And I was about to say something else that is weighing heavily on my mind. I can't remember what it was.

She set the day's report down on his desk.

— There it is, the *Sixth Mass Extinction Report*, he said to clarify what she had given him.

— Then you had a call from Mr. Elrod. He informed us that tomorrow morning a maintenance crew will be going out to the lake protection site.

— He said that? Tomorrow morning? Then that's how this is going to be. That man would take over the world if it were for the taking.

— He wanted to know if there was information that we might want to send them.

— Information, yes, send them the reports, the notes I made the other day on the Plovers. Send them along. Except for the sections to do with our research, that they shouldn't have. Early tomorrow morning? Fine. All right. Then let them know I'll be there myself. I'll put in an appearance to show how much I care.

She was about to leave.

— But one more thing because if what I'm thinking, I'm not sure if I can say what it is. Then isn't it amazing what we will think about when we could just as well be doing something else at the same time? Or is it not surprising that if there is a better alternative, that we would not think of that first? I guess I would like to ask you a personal question about myself, and it is something I would not want to ask myself is how personal it is. That doesn't sound right: to be asking a personal question about oneself to someone else. It doesn't make sense. Never mind. I'm going to go up to the roof. I'll be up on the roof. Why not? That is the only reason to do anything any more, because, why not? I can't think of another or better reason.

He went up to the roof and he waited for Isa Martin de Aguilera to come along. When she came he asked her if she wouldn't mind if he were to ask her a personal question about himself, and since she was going to include him in her memoirs then it might be of interest to her.

— You look terrible, Harold.

— I do. Because I had too much to drink last night. I'm still drunk probably. My stomach is unsettled, it's not going to leave me in peace. I could be violently ill at a moment's notice. Then Isa, events are getting out of hand. I got drunk last night and Karol shared with me design ideas that she is working on for a prison, she did, as I was going to sleep, she was telling me about it. So there's the town minister, who lost his church, a man of faith, who no longer may have it. He has lost his faith that he has had probably since he could remember. I went out drinking with him. I got liquored with a vicar. Can you believe it? Then I got home and Karol presented me with a bill for the costly damages for our catastrophic wedding reception party to remind me of how I regret that fateful day not long ago when I gave my life away for a pittance. It's a lot of money, a great amount of money. A loan will maybe be required to pay it off. It will take years to pay the loan off. Then she spoke to me about the plans she's making for how people will be locked away in cells for years on end. But tell me now, is it possible that I'm not who I pretend to be, and for a reason that I'm not aware of I drank too much to forget who I was or who I am?

— You haven't forgotten.

— But really is there nothing to stop us from doing what we have to do except disinterest or the fear of doing nothing.

— Harold, I can't listen to this. I have work to do.

— Let us talk a little more.

— We have to work. You have work to do.

— I do. Today I received the *Sixth Mass Extinction Report* to work on, he said grimly.

— You have too much to do.

— Then I'll read it and I'll come up here and leap over the edge. I hope it is well-written. And Isa, what if someone is out to get me?

The Unorthodox Ox

Thankfully I know it's not you.

— Don't be so sure about that.

She said to him, if need be, they could talk later, except if he were inclined to be so damn bloody-minded.

He went down to his office. He opened up the report.

The introductory conclusion of the *Sixth Mass Extinction Report* began: *It is happening due to the expansion of agricultural land, the building of towns and cities and transport infrastructure that joins them, the uncontrolled exploitation of resources, rising populations, improper disposal of wastes, that the earth's capacity to sustain its biological heritage is failing. Then it appears evident by present estimations that at the present rate of extinction within thirty years one fifth of all species will die. 17,000 to 100,000 species will disappear annually. And this decline is occurring at an accelerated rate in comparison to previous mass extinctions which had transpired over periods of tens of thousands of years.*

Then what we know, is that this environmental abnormality; i.e., mankind's dominance cannot continue forever, and as environmental abnormalities do, will correct itself. So what is then occurring is likely a natural process whereby it has to be inevitable that intelligence in the wrong species is foreordained to be a fatal flaw and perhaps a law of evolution is that intelligence extinguishes itself, but if not a "law" maybe it is a common consequence. Then our concern is to see if this consequence is inevitably preordained.

He read to the end of the *Sixth Mass Extinction Report*. Then he returned to the roof and he looked around in all directions and far down at the ground far below, and he waited and waited for Isa to come and join him.

— What are we doing up here already? he asked her.

— The usual.

— I read the report.

— I am sure you did.

— So what do you think? Do you think? Do you think it's possible that we are too intelligent for our own good?

They laughed hardily.

— What an idiot I am, a consummate fool. Excuse me for being so self-absorbed.

— I wouldn't go so far as to say consummate. You have a ways to go before becoming a consummate fool. That requires a degree of expertise.

— You agree with me, but don't agree with me too readily.

— Yes and no.

— You are or are you not in agreement?

— I might be or I might not be. You'll never know.

— Then we don't know if we are too intelligent for our own good. Which is further evidence of our innate stupidity. How depressing is such a thought.

— Yet obvious.

— It is not a happy thought. It is a maddening one.

— If you think about it too much.

— We ought not to, anyway Isa, you can understand that I have a good reason to take a break and get away for a while, I do, because of these frustrations that I'm harbouring, they're getting the better of me. So there are these problems that cannot be resolved, not with intelligence, not with common sense or rationally, and if we're being foolish that doesn't help to improve matters.

— Harold, you think too much. Think less.

— That is easily said. How are we supposed to do that when we're the most intelligent of all the animals?

— Do not ask how.

— You're right. That's an intelligent idea.

He was leaving for the day.

Then he saw there was no longer a stuffed frog sitting in the parking booth window. He was not to ask why.

As he was driving home he was listening to Bach violin concertos, and during the second movement of the concerto No. 2 in E Major for violin and orchestra BWV 1042 he found himself to be better off than he might have thought was humanly possible.

§

They were leaning back sitting upright against the headboard. They were thanking one another for what was naturally relaxing.

Then they were going over their plans for what they had to look forward to from the trip north. He described to her in more detail the remoteness of the location. He said what they would do, whenever they wanted as they pleased. They would walk on trails in the woods, swim in lakes, bird watch, as it was the time of the southern migrations that would be gathering together.

They were fantasizing about the coming week that they were to spend in the remote north, and he was to blow the experience out of proportion literally by taking out a duck caller he had brought along, and he blew on the duck caller with measured enthusiasm.

— Now we can multiply this sound for what will be thousands of calling ducks and geese that will be congregating for their migration. It gets noisy. I should like to warn you how noisy it can get. Tens of thousands of geese can make themselves heard like few other birds who take to the skies.

— It isn't going to be a problem? she knew.

— It shouldn't be if we're appreciative of it.

He blew on the caller again for her appreciation of it.

— We'll call them down and some of them will land at our feet, and we'll wish for them to have a safe journey as they head off south for the long winter.

The different duck calls that he knew how to make he demonstrated for her: the basic call, the greeting call with seven notes fading out, the feed call, the hail or highball call, the comeback call, the lonesome hen call, the pleading or begging hail call, and whistling, and when she blew on the caller as instructed he told her that he had just come down himself and had landed at her feet. He was on his knees.

Then they were blowing the caller for each other to come down to one another's feet. They were looking forward to the trip north.

— So Mary-Adeline, I might have mentioned to you that I had given that broach previously to my wife as a present, she had refused it, and had she noticed you wearing it at the demolition. Imagine the scene, what I would have said.

— That'd have been tricky.

— I'd have confessed on the spot. Then with my mother-in-law present. You would have been in an awkward position. I'd have defended you with my life though.

— Against your wife or against your mother-in-law?

— We could have run off together in the rain, and with the crumbled church in the background. It would have been inspiring.

— The broach is mine now though?

— I promise it is yours.

What was the knock-on effect of the dung-beetle's role in inspiring hope she alluded to.

— So why did I marry her you might ask me? What was I thinking? I'd have to answer that by saying that we were to have been an upstanding couple. But the truth is, we decided our habits were familiar and we owed one another something, and I had given up on my reservations. But I escaped every so often. I'd run away, but I always went back to her. Until finally I decided to forget about what I was holding out for. What a misguided decision that was. Around the same time I had almost fallen off a cliff. Then maybe I thought I was lucky to be alive and that was enough. Though I am fond of her mother. If she had been her mother I'd have married her.

— She seemed like a friendly woman.

— We met on a ferryboat on a crossing in the Aegean Sea. She wanted to introduce her daughter to me after finding out what she needed to know. Then from the moment we met my instincts had alerted me to what turned out to be the case. So wouldn't it be more sensible to follow one's instincts and trust them? And had I dedicated myself to a life of research in the field and lived happily and honourably and pursued my interests. There is a tendency to be fooled. If we could trust our instincts. And it occurs to me that something will only be done afterwards when it is too late in most instances.

— That is usually true.

He was wondering and asked if she had suffered from unexpected setbacks in her plans along the way. They were not terrible. She had been grateful for the talent and fortune that she had been blessed with.

— I've always known what I was listening for and I imagine what I hear perfectly, though it's different when I play. Then I've always wanted to live for harmony and for what goes together.

He agreed with her.

— It's that simple, it is, but never easy, it is never easy, it's difficult, in fact, she said.

She made a meal for him. It was light and settled his stomach. Then as he was leaving he told her what it was like to walk in the front door at home and experience a few mixed feelings, but no remorse whatsoever.

— I wouldn't want to be the one to keep you? she asked.

— Or would you be the one to keep me?

He blew his caller for her. He went home.

§

As on that other night he could not bring himself to go immediately inside, and so he went for a walk down the same country road to the end of it.

In the distant houses the lights were off. There were no stars nor a moon. A wind had died. It was a quiet dark and cool night. He was ill-dressed for the chill. When he arrived back he was cold. But even then he would have preferred to have stayed outside. Yet he went in. Then he sat down in the living room to warm and cheer himself up with some other variation on his predicament. He got himself something to drink. That was when she came down the stairs and into the kitchen.

— There you are, she said.

He gestured to her how he was uninterested in saying too much.

— I heard you drive up a while ago, Harold.

— Yes.

— What are you doing?

— I'm having something to drink.

— It isn't surprising you're thirsty.

She asked if he had had anything to eat and asked why had he come home so late when she had told him to come home early.

— You might have called to tell me you were going to be late. I left a message for you.

— I didn't listen to it.

— You didn't. Why not?

— I thought I wouldn't.

She had made a meal for them.

— You haven't eaten?

He did not answer.

— I can heat up what I made for you.

— I'll be hungry tomorrow.

— You can suit yourself.

He thought he might. He retired upstairs. She followed behind him.

— You had a bad day?

— Not entirely, he said.

— You ought to ask me how my day was.

— How was your day, Karol?

— It wasn't good either. Then you don't want my understanding, but I'm hoping for yours. I had a rough day. The *Inside Justice Tour* was unpleasant. It was terrible really. I didn't think it was going to be so disturbing. It was inhumane.

— That's too bad.

— It was awful, just awful.

— You were expecting something else.

— When walking down along a corridor of a cell block the inmates were threatening us and screaming obscenities. I won't tell you what they said.

— Unflattering words.

— I don't know what I expected, Harold.

— You were expecting it to be less inhumane.

— It was brutal.

— You expect that if we lock people up like animals that it wouldn't be inhumane, not that we can say why we lock up animals and that that isn't inhumane.

— I don't know what I expected.

— You expected them to welcome you into their midst?

— Have you gone and got drunk? Are you drunk?

— You were expecting that those you were visiting would be pleased to have the chance to meet you? They were going to invite you into their cells for a chat and to tell you about their hopes and dreams? Were you hoping they would appreciate that you were to be building a home for their friends? So then you were asking to be acknowledged as an architect and to be afforded respect because you are a free woman? And then to be seen to be superior for who you are and for what you do? That's what you were expecting.

— Maybe I wasn't expecting that.

He undressed himself.

— What were you expecting?

The Unorthodox Ox

— Nothing that you would understand evidently.

— That later when you came home that I would understand how you felt because those imprisoned men rejected you?

— That would be asking too much, she was raising her voice.

— I think it would be, that you were and are asking too much. He took up his pyjamas.

— Then would you brush yourself?

— You are expecting me to brush myself.

— God, sometimes you disgust me, Harold.

— You are disgusted all of a sudden.

— It isn't so sudden.

— I have made you into someone who is suddenly and easily disgusted or who always has been.

— I might thank you on that account.

— You might as well, go ahead. Thank me if you have nothing better to do.

— Maybe those men got what they deserved. Judging by their bad behaviour, it looked like it. Maybe all of you should be locked up.

He was brushing himself. He thrashed about before her. She watched amused. He showered.

He got into bed.

— Look Harold, we don't have to be like this. I'm sorry. I didn't mean what I was saying. I was upset. I was mad that you were late, and that you didn't call me, she said.

— It's all right, there is no need to apologize, there isn't.

— I didn't mean it. I am sorry. So I hope you are not too tired now?

She was suggesting what might have temporarily put to rest the argument that they were always having. He said, she was right, he was tired. So then as expected his response was unsatisfactory and unacceptable to her and she read him the riot act that she had been working on for so many years, but it was as she was going to tell him what she wanted to discuss with him that he just got up out of the bed to leave the room and to go downstairs and sleep on a couch and escape having to participate in what the discussion was to lead to. But she had guessed what he was up to and she went downstairs after him and she demanded that he return to bed or he would rue the rest of his days. Her threat he gave into, and he was hoping not to have to discuss what she might have meant by it, but she was going to tell him what she meant by it regardless.

He went back upstairs. He got back into bed and said that he was ready to go to sleep. But without giving him a moment's rest she got onto what was the cause of the problems they were experiencing. He thought that they did not need to go into it further at that time. He had been as patient as he was going to be, he was exhausted, he tried again to explain to her, and she went on to say all of what she probably wanted to say and more and then after the niggling kind of quarrelling that he had wanted to avoid, he was at wit's end. He couldn't stand it any more. He lost his reason. He blurted out.

— I can't put up with this. I can't go on like this any more. So I want you to know, Karol. Guess what?! You'll never guess. You won't. I'm having an affair, an extramarital affair, behind your back, right behind your back, under your very nose. I am. Yes, I am. Now you know. Are you happy? Are you happy now?

Then without making any unconvincing excuses he told her that he was involved in an affair that he was enjoying and that was the explanation for his absence at dinner and his other absences, and he thought to mention that he was having the time of his life and he told her that it was not a mere passing fancy. It was not that. It was not. It was much more than that. He was in love and he was hoping to continue to fall more in love with the other woman. But of course, she did not believe him. She laughed at him, laughed altogether uproariously. She did not believe him in the least. There was no reason to. Then it was his word against hers and she accused him of resorting to a fantasy in order to win the argument, which is what he was doing, because in fact he didn't know what he is doing really, did he? But he asked her to consider his behaviour: how he had been late coming home, why he was moody, why he eluded her advances, and if she didn't want to believe it she could maybe pick up on what was another woman's fragrance that was lingering on him and it had seeped into the pores of his skin, and it wouldn't matter how hard he were to brush his epidermis.

— The smell on you is alcohol, Harold!

Then she complained of him wanting to hurt her feelings, but he had to have known that she was not to be fooled. Nevertheless, she was bothered enough by the intent of what he had said to leave the room herself, and she was the one to get up and go down to sleep on the couch. Then she said as she was running out of the room and down the stairs.

— It is a good thing I'm going away.

— The sooner the better.

— Yes, if you want to find someone to have an affair with, go right ahead.

— Is that your blessing?

— I would pity that woman.

The sound of her crying lulled him to sleep. He had a sound night's sleep.

§

He woke up in the morning from what was a recurring dream that he had never remembered entirely and it was the unresolved end of that dream that had given him a sense of it being always familiar. But that morning he remembered the end.

It was as usual, he had been flying along through the sky under his own steam at a high speed through the clouds. A falling trail of blood was draining out through the soles of his feet, which had always caused him to lose consciousness, and it was because of this: the fainting in his dream that explained why he had always forgotten it. He had reasoned. But that morning he was waking up as he was beginning to faint and before the last drop of blood had left him, before he had started to pass out and fall like lead from the sky, and he almost seemed to realize what was happening in his dream, which was promising.[1]

There was her message waiting for him: *I want to tell you what we have to do to avoid so much unnecessary conflict, Harold,* was its title. The thesis being what they would have to do and likewise what the effort was that they would have to make to get things right. Then there was a completed *Frogwatch Observation Form* for him

---

1   *A related non-recurring dream*
It had been a fine night to have had a good sleep and he had slept with no concern for what he was to forget might have or not have happened when he woke up, as if not having fallen asleep to begin with the night before.

to take away. So she had gone out and monitored the frogs without him and returned home, and she had written and electronically sent her message and she had left the house early for work leaving him to his own devices, so that he might dispute her recommendations without her having to be around to listen to his objections.

In her message she had pointed out to him that it was important that they both admit how they were both to blame, and so it made sense that they work on solutions together and do what they could to iron out their differences maybe once and for all. Although that meant that he would have to do more himself, if he would, without her always having to tell him what the problem was. *Because the consequences of you not taking care of your problems. We know what they are.*

She had singled out that his exaggerations were not helpful, then moreover, she suggested that he could be more reasonable and flexible and not do unto others as he would not do unto himself. Then he should try to do what he had to do to help himself, and there was only so much she could do to help him in that regard. So maybe then he would be less resentful if he were to do his part without her having to meddle in the difficult side of his personality.

The completed *Frogwatch Observation Form* had not recorded a change from recent monitorings, which indicated an unwillingness on her part to notice a change in the cooling temperatures of the season.

§

He came up from out of the riverbed. He walked out onto the pebbled beach.

Down the beach along rows of newly erected fence posts there were workers unrolling wood slat fencing. They were then nailing the fencing up onto the posts.

There was a surveyor that went up to him. The man introduced himself and provided information for what was being done. Councillor Elrod was to arrive soon, he said.

The surveyor then told him that there were mistakes that had been made, as were recorded in the original survey, as for where the fence boundary was to go and when verifying the measurements

The Unorthodox Ox

through a distance meter the mistakes were evident.

— We corrected it, the surveyor said to him.

Harold looked through a laser rangefinder to see what the problem had been.

— Thank you, it is a good thing to get things right when we can, when we are able to, he said to the surveyor.

He walked down the beach by the water's edge. He was looking to see if he might find evidence of Piping Plovers.

There was a Sandhill Crane *(Grus canadensis)* slowly circling over and around the lake, not a related species to Piping Plovers. He watched the crane gliding effortlessly through the air, and he understood how relaxing that must be. Bird-down was embedded in the pebbles on the shore.

He was looking back in time and it might have seemed that he was returning in his thoughts to the past to when he would have had a view of things that would have been different than the present one in how he might ever have imagined.

Councillor Elrod arrived. The hammering appeared to stop to welcome him.

Then it was from where they saw each other, that they were far enough away to have been at the near opposite ends of humanity, but they were closer than either of them suspected.

They met at an unfenced post that both were to get support from when alternatively leaning on it.

In the instant they said hello a worker struck a finger with a blow of a hammer. The man screamed out in pain.

— I should like to thank you for coming out, and I thank you for the reports you sent along to us, said Mr. Elrod.

— I wanted to be helpful and offer some advice.

— We're taking care of it as you see.

— It looks like it.

— Though I imagine you've come out here regarding the occurrence of the other night. You know my wife and I did not appreciate your late visit. It was obvious you had been drinking.

— I had been, but I'm sober now.

— You should not have come at such a late hour.

— I would not have under normal circumstances.

— So you might be interested to know that there have been

rumours circulating about you. Did you know that?

— Is that right?

— All right, it's regrettable what happened. I understand you have reason to be displeased for good reason.

— I'm hoping there will be a fairer evaluation for what the damages amounted to and I should like to believe that this is not out-an-out exploitation of some kind, coercion, or that I am being swindled by interests under your authority.

— No, it is what it has to be, I'm afraid.

— You said that and I said we would seek legal council if necessary.

— Which would be a miscalculation on your part.

— I would like to believe that we'd be better off to come to an equitable agreement.

— I would recommend that you not consider the litigious route because I can promise that undertaking legal proceedings will result in legal expenses that will exceed the present amount that you're liable for. And consider that we take no issue in wearing out and exhausting those who enter into legal disputes with us. The process is slow and drawn out, for as long as it takes. Time is on our side and not on the side of the claimant. Then our lawyers are paid on commission. They're highly motivated and if we need to pay them more we raise taxes or issue municipal bonds. Sometimes we hire detectives to conduct investigations. A good private-eye knows how to follow up on rumours. And you see, with what are unlimited resources it is not difficult to annihilate someone who is looking for trouble.

— That's how works?

— It works well.

— I see.

— Then I might suggest that you'd want to avoid other grievances that might come up. So I had a visit from my neighbour who saw you on my doorstep. He asked me about filing a complaint for the disturbance. And your own neighbour has been talking to people apparently. Ms. Brown said something about you running around undressed in front of your house. Then if you're interested to see what we are capable of, I can refer you to those who lost out and have nothing to show for their pains.

The Unorthodox Ox

The Councillor gave the fence post a shaking to see how the cement had set.

— Then I guess we can assume that we won't be renting the municipal community hall out to you in the future for receptions or funerals, Mr. Elrod laughed victoriously.

He ordered the man who had hurt himself to get back to work.

— So my men are doing their job. But it is important to keep an eye on them. Human beings are indolent creatures by nature. Then what is there to do to get the Piping Plovers to return?

— We wait.

— I'd have thought there was something.

— We wait.

— There is no reason for them not to? It would be a shame if we were wasting our time.

— They will come back in their own due time. What I sent to you explained that.

— Well, come back out here to see the work when it is completed. Then our surveyor found a mistake that your people made.

— He informed me of that.

— Anyway, I must see what my men are up to.

Harold walked away. He went down into the river-bed.

There were lines of slow-moving traffic that slowed him down, and he was at his leisure as he was driving, which had been given to him by the presence of others over the miles, by others who shouldn't have been in a hurry either to get where they had to be for whatever reason.

§

In his office at his desk he got out a letter to read. It had to have been one of the first letters before dating, organizing, and filing them.

Then to begin, he was trying to remember how much of what he remembered had changed since that time, for better or worse, or was going to be always the same perhaps. Everything was going to be the same, always almost the same or maybe always worse.

He flattened the paper out onto his desk. He turned on his desk lamp. He remarked upon the water spots that were from his dry tears.

Dear you and me, dear us,

We should not to be asking questions, because who knows if we don't? Which is a question that we have to ask but not answer. But then here we are. We have not resigned. Yet why didn't we throw in the towel before getting wet? But we've continued on, believing that if we are swimming in a sea infested with sharks that we must keep swimming and it is better to risk the humiliation of being torn to shreds by elasmobranches than to allow oneself to drown. But maybe not now, that is not how it is. Maybe it's time to get out of the water. So either get out or kill yourself or jump off a roof or over a cliff. Or you could run your head straight through an impenetrable brick wall. If you don't, you're on your own, and I want nothing more to do with you.

Yet still, love until the end of your days and until then, Godspeed.

Your one and only, forever,

Lost soul

Then if his soul had once written such an unforgiving and timely letter of resignation that would have been an indication of the kind of reactionary, ornery, and abject rascal his own spirit had always been.

So that file, *Letters of Resignation,* it was a thick folder that contained countless pages and a number of the letters, he and Isa Martin de Aguilera had written together, starting out from when they had begun working. They had written letters of resignation to amuse themselves and to air problems they were working on that they believed needed to be examined from a resigned vantage point. She had said that collated they would have been an accurate chronicle, a memoir of their work together.

Then on his own, for the sake of entertainment, he had gone as far as to have written several embarrassingly introspective suicide notes that said goodbye to the mean and cruel world.

So having read his soul's letter of resignation he thought that he would have a look at one of his irresolute suicide notes, and he got out one he thought he remembered that his soul also had contributed to and who when younger had admonished him for considering such an ignoble idea and he had wisely advised him that he had better be sure of what he was up to, or he would be sorry because there's no turning back when it's all over and done with, and if taking one's life, the same as when in love, there is no room for error in making larger-than-life mistakes, "Get it right or forget about it and don't forget, you can't win in this world and it's a dead man's game when it's over." But why did his soul care about love or death when he was so cowardly immortal?

But for the soul, no matter where on a time-line he might be, it makes no difference where, because it is a continuum for the souls of this world. But suppose that this has to do with the new modern and futuristic incarnation of a soul, who is on the forward side of past romantic traditions and influences, and he's a kind of free spirit and so he is in the process of losing or has already lost his humanity and is bound to separate from his once earthly attachments is how he will end up, but then like the modern man that he represents, he is rotten to the core.

Then knowing that the modern day soul is lacking in conviction and is short-sighted, indifferent, lazy, uncharitable, spineless, feckless, void of honest or modest feeling, humourless, sexless, artless, and a nervous wreck. Knowing this! Perhaps it isn't so terrible to be soulless in the end. But he at that time wasn't interested in such hopelessness, as he was in love and bubbling in a stew of passion, and all those many dejected souls out there could be damned for the ages for all he cared.

He balled up the old suicide note and tossed it in the garbage.

§

The day's report for him to work on, the *Land Migratory Bird Report (LMBR)* was on the change of bird migratory trajectories and on the species and the numbers that were lost when migrating. It accounted for what happens to migratory birds after they swoop down from the sky one last time and never fly again.

The arrival on his desk of the *(LMBR)* could not have been less than a hitherto unknown coincidence, as he was so relatively engaged with the subjects of love, life, and death, and how birds had been an undying interest for him and so many were dying though meant to live and thrive.

He started to read through the *(LMBR)* and he identified with what he was certainly aware of but had never been too unquestionably sure about and he was indulging in the themes—that he was reviewing and that similar to what had seemed to be happening to himself—they were running away on him and so he was carrying on with more than he could get a comprehensive grasp of. But it was then, that it was by the unveiling order of events, a phone call interrupted him.

On the other end of the line was a man, who in introducing himself stated his position, his title as: Bishop of the diocese. He was a friend of George's and he was calling to tell him what had happened to his friend. That from the day after the church had come down he had gone on a binge. His colleague was in hospital.

— He's experiencing a difficult and painful withdrawal from his addiction.

The Bishop explained how he was an old and dear friend, and he had an explanation for what had occurred.

— He suffers from a serious chronic illness, but we all have our crosses to bear.

The old friend explained what were the concerns of those who were the old friends.

— For those of us who know him well we hope that when he recovers and is better that he will be able and willing to continue to involve himself in his charity work, he's always been one to help others. Then now he is the one who is in need of help. And so what happened will become common knowledge. He was involved in a barroom dispute and he helped to resolve the differences between those who were in disagreement. Then to thank him for intervening, those he had helped bought him drinks, as such people do. So he ended up in hospital. He asked me to call a few people to tell them what happened. He said you were with him that night.

It had to have seemed to have been the right thing to do to offer to pay George a visit in the hospital. The Bishop said his friend would appreciate that, and he said he thought that in those circumstances that it was possible that not everyone who knew him would see fit to pay a visit.

— I will see him when I'm able, and he is in need of our help and support in his hour of need.

The old Bishop gave the time for what were the hospital afternoon and evening visiting hours.

— God willing one day, he will learn to control himself. He has to get treatment. It would be hard to get him in for it. It is a difficult illness to beat. Might I inquire if you suffer from the affliction?

Harold said no he did not. He thanked the Bishop for calling to notify him.

Off he went to speak with Isa and to beg for her indulgence. He was in need of it. He was in need of the indulgence that she might have afforded him.

— My, my, Harold, she tried to reassure him.

— I suspect that this is what might happen to those of faith when their beliefs turn out irrefutably to be bunk. They give up under the strain. They fall apart. But there's no way of knowing how bad off someone like that will be without his faith.

— No, there isn't.

— I couldn't have known.

— Not if you were drunk at the time. She chuckled.

— I couldn't have known he was going to go on a protracted binge. I couldn't have known.

— Not if you say so.

— I was too drunk myself to have known, you're right.

— He didn't know himself maybe. Alcoholics are often not willing to admit how serious their sickness is.

— I didn't get him to leave with me. I didn't take him home. I should have. What if I am blamed for what happened? I think that that is what that Bishop was intimating.

— You might be.

— I was too drunk myself to get him to come with me. But I asked him to come along. I didn't insist. What can I say to anyone who asks me why I didn't take him home? If family and friends ask why I didn't see fit to make sure he got safely home. Those who would mistakenly want to blame me would be right to do so? If they're at the hospital and decide to take me to task for not having done what a reasonable and decent person would have done.

— That wouldn't be right.

— If I think so why wouldn't someone else?

— Don't visit then.

— I said I would. I don't know why I said that. I didn't know

139

what else to say. I shall visit him, as I'm curious. I'll want to know if I am going to be blamed. I would want to know. I would want to know that.

— You would.

— Wouldn't you?

— Would you like me to come with you to the hospital?

— You're curious too? You would be.

— I'll come with you.

— Then the church was destroyed and the man. I did nothing in either instance. What kind of low-life am I? What sort of unconscionable evil am I capable of? I am as bad as a tyrant who has committed human atrocities? I wonder.

— For God's sake what is it that will satisfy you?

— I'm losing my faith myself, too? No, I never had any. You are asking me what would make me happy. There are a few things that would. Love makes me happy. That and living in a utopia. I've always thought that would be nice. I wouldn't mind that. As long as I wasn't the man called upon to make sure everything works perfectly. If I am amusing you, I'd be happy for that, which seems to be something that I might be having trouble with of late.

— You bemuse me.

— That pleases me then.

— And Harold, you've reminded me of someone who used to live in a neighbourhood where I lived, who was referred to as the abominable man, that might have been his real name for all anyone knew. He was indefensible as you would like to be. He brought out the worst in people. The kids in the neighbourhood when they saw him threw rocks at him. No one thought to do anything to stop them from trying to stone him to death. Everyone would have thrown rocks at him and at his wife if we could have got away with it. They went about in orange clothes, pants, shirts, shoes, orange, head to foot. I had it against them like everyone. I was no different than anyone else. We disapproved of them for how orange they looked. No one could stand the sight of them as they went about arm in arm calling attention to themselves every day. For some reason they were impossible to ignore. But why did we care? It shouldn't have made any difference. Then I saw him one day in a pair of orange shorts in the winter and I realized we shouldn't waste time on those

The Unorthodox Ox

kinds of abominable men. We have to ignore them. Let them do as they please, whatever they want.

— We're the victims no matter what.

— So I'll come with you.

— You don't have to.

— I don't, but I do.

— No.

— I am going with you, as you are in need of female guile.

— If you put it that way. I can't refuse you.

He thanked her.

— Then Isa, earlier I was reading over an old letter of resignation, but I don't know why.

— Wasting time? Let's get to work.

In working through the *Land Migratory Bird Report* that was in need of only a few corrections; he noted in the northerly and southerly mapped pathways and in the conclusion and the predictions, how there was no suggestion to the effect that old routes could be returned to and there was no way to go back to an earlier and different point of departure, somewhere else, and figuratively the moral high road was no longer the road it once was meant to be, but it was a narrow and winding path and the passing roadside scenery was not then to necessarily delight the senses and a good feeling of knowing how to survive with unpredictable outcomes was as confused as ever, as were his thoughts, as they were, but were somehow clear in the mind, though troubling, yet clear as could be, which was in stark contrast to reality itself, and that may have been a blessing in disguise.

He looked after the work he had to take care of for the day. Uneventfully it passed.

He told Isa again that she didn't have to accompany him. It was enough for her to have offered.

— I'm the one who is going to judge you, she said.

So their day's work while going to the hospital they discussed.

— I was reading the *(LMBR)*, and it occurred to me that if things keep on like this who knows where we're heading.

— Onward, she said.

Doctors, nurses, patients, and administrators were outside at the main entrance discussing minor or serious illnesses. Some were smoking.

They were going along the corridors to find their way. Harold met a man he had to have known who was upset about some terrible and tragic news.

— I've no idea who he was and I wasn't going to ask him what the problem was.

— I was afraid you were going to, Isa said.

At a nursing station the attending nurse took down their names. She informed them of the hospital regulations. She instructed them how to handle her patient. They were to not overexcite him. He needed to rest. They were to try and raise his spirits. Needless to say it was important regardless of the desperation of the patient's pleas. They were not to provide him with abusive substances. One would not be surprised how often that happened, the nurse told them. Specific questions they might have had, the visitor who was with him could answer for them.

Trudi Brown opened the door, and she whispered that he was asleep, as was evident by the sound of laboured breathing coming from the bed. He had just fallen asleep.

Harold offered to come back another time. Ms. Brown agreed that that would be best. But there was movement in the bed, a phlegmatic cough. George called out. She quietly asked for him to go back to sleep.

— I heard you telling them to go away? What are you trying to do, Brown? Are you trying to get on my nerves?

He had a coughing fit that woke him up.

— She wants to send you packing? Don't let her terrorize you. But she wouldn't hurt a flee. She's just an old pussy cat really.

She asked him if he was all right, and she attended to his coughing. She cleaned up what he had coughed up. They stepped into the room. He told her that he was fine and that she knew he always coughed when he woke up. It was normal, she knew that and she didn't have to make an unnecessary stink about it.

He invited them to make themselves at home. They positioned themselves near the foot of the bed.

— You didn't bring flowers, and it's like a florist in here. But something to drink would have been nice. Excuse me, I was dozing. So then Trudi was reading *The Songs of Solomon* to me and I nodded off.

— They weren't going to bring you anything to drink, you know that, George.

— Someone might.

— The nurses took away the rubbing alcohol, she said to them.

— You can't expect a person to believe that, and you don't believe that yourself, he said to her.

— I believe it. I asked them to.

— You didn't ask them to take away the rubbing alcohol, don't be kidding with me. One drink to take the edge off is all I'm asking for.

— It is forbidden, George.

— Relief is forbidden? I wonder if my ears are my own to hear you say that relief is forbidden. From you of all people to say that, you old hussy.

He had another fit of coughing. She affectionately rubbed his tired old back.

— If I am going to suffer like this, should I not be allowed to enjoy myself while I'm at it? Which is what I always wanted. And Harold, do me favour, can you get me a bottle of scotch? She is not going to. All right, I admit I've had more than my fair share of the sacramental wine. But it's cruel to leave me here like this. I shouldn't have to suffer more than I am. I won't go on a mad tear. If I have too much you can take it away from me. You can ask that nurse to take it away. And there is a special place in hell for her I can tell you.

— When I come back I'll sneak something in for you, he said.

— A single malt whiskey would go down nicely. I am fond of cognac, too. Cognac is always good for throat congestion, and once I drank an expensive bottle of cognac on one occasion worth several hundreds of dollars I found out afterwards. I don't remember where or when that was, but I remember the taste, a smooth taste, smoky and warm, like an elixir. I was at a conference. I was on a train somewhere, on a train, on my way to a conference. I spoke at a lot of conferences. I usually had a few to loosen up. It must have been at a conference. I went to so many it is not surprising I've forgotten. I don't think I'm losing my marbles. So how do I appear? But it doesn't matter what I look like any more really.

He was pale. His cheeks were swollen. His voice sounded weak, but had resonated when asking for a drink.

— Who are you, Miss? I have never seen you before in my life that I know.

Isa said she shouldn't have been intruding probably.

— No, I am always happy to meet someone who I would like to get to know, he said.

Then she expressed her regards and thought to mention how her own father had a drinking problem, but he had been a good and hardworking man despite his weakness, she said.

— Yes, let me say, that I suspect that one of the most difficult things to do is to enjoy life and know how to live. Few know how to live. It is where I failed. I know I haven't enjoyed myself enough, not as I could have. And when I think of the opportunities that I passed up, what slipped through my fingers and out of my grasp. Though there were other times when I exercised no restraint, no restraint whatsoever. I was a glutton and gluttony is a sin. It is not as bad as some of the other sins, but it's a sin. Excuse me, I have a morbid fascination for that subject, theoretically, practically, scientifically, and poetically.

Trudi handed him a glass of water.

— I should have married you when I had the chance. So would you read some more? Read for us, would you?

— Later George.

— Read to us.

— Your visitors are here to visit. You want them to visit with you.

— You can read for them, too.

— They don't want to hear me read. You want to visit with them. She winked at them to let them know how she was humouring him.

— Trudi has the voice of a saint. Then would you not like to hear an Irish saint singing *The Songs of Solomon*? You know, I think your father had to have been a priest. You didn't know who he was and your mother was very young. It's possible.

They would gladly listen to her read, they said.

— You want to play hard to get. You always liked to play hard to get. But you were a push over, Brown.

— I only was for you, George.

— I am fond of *The Songs of Solomon* that I never read in a service. Because it would be impossible without the intent coming through. Then in a service the effect of that would be contrary to the idea of religious solemnity.

— All right, if that is what you want, but you have to rest then, she said.

— I could do that, he said.

The retired teacher sat down in the bedside chair. She took up a pair of reading glasses, she placed them onto her nose. She adjusted her posture. She pulled her bearing together and she regained something lost from when she was a younger woman and running free and wild on the bogs of Ireland.

On the other side of a curtain another man in the room groaned, "God help me."

— I could read to you later, she said.

— Read to us, he bleated.

— But you have to rest then.

— Yes, I am a little tired.

She opened a Bible and held it up, she winked at them again, and she began to read at the height of it.

— *Behold, thou art fair my love; behold, thou art fair; thou hast doves' eyes within thy locks: thy hair is as a flock of goats, that appear from Mount Gilead.*

Thy teeth are like a flock of sheep that are even shorn, which came up from the washing; whereof every one bear twins, and none is barren among them.

Thy lips are like a thread of scarlet, and thy speech is comely: thy temples are like a piece of a pomegranate within thy locks.

Thy neck is like the tower of David builded for an armoury, whereon there hang a thousand bucklers, all shields of mighty men.

Thy two breasts are like two young roes that are twins, which feed among the lilies.

She paused to see if she would continue.

— Embrace those fine words, George said.

She proclaimed louder.

— *Until the day break, and the shadows flee away, I will get me to the mountain of myrrh, and to the hill of frankincense.*

Thou art all fair, my love; there is no spot in thee.

Come with me from Lebanon, my spouse, with me from Leba-

non: look from the top of Amana, from the top of Shenir and Hermon, from the lions' dens, from the mountains of the leopards.

Thou hast ravished my heart, my sister, my spouse; thou hast ravished my heart with one of thine eyes, with one chain of thy neck.

How fair is thy love, my sister, my spouse! how much better is thy love than wine! and the smell of thine ointments than all spices!

— Better than wine, he said.

— *Thy lips, Oh my spouse, drop as the honeycomb: honey and milk are under thy tongue; and the smell of thy garments is like the smell of Lebanon.*

A garden enclosed is my sister, my spouse; a spring shut up, a fountain sealed.

Thy plants are an orchard of pomegranates, with pleasant fruits; camphire, with spikenard,

Spikenard and saffron; calamus and cinnamon, with all trees of frankincense; myrrh and aloes, with all the chief spices: A fountain of gardens, a well of living waters, and streams from Lebanon.

Awake, O north wind; and come, thou south; blow upon my garden, that the spices thereof may flow out. Let my beloved come into his garden, and eat his pleasant fruits.

Trudi dried his watery eyes. He thanked her.

— You're welcome, she said kindly.

— The theosophy of that is open to interpretation. Some say it's an allegory for the love of God. But I think that's far-fetched. "Thou art all fair, my love; there is no spot in thee." That is a very nice thing to say. I'd like to say that to you, Dear.

He slumped to one side of the bed and he asked.

— What time is it? Where's my watch? Why has my watch been taken from me? I don't know what time it is. Read some more.

— That's enough for now, sleep now.

— We'll let you rest, Harold said.

— I think I'll rest. Scotch it will be then? Harold, I am counting on you.

— I'll see what I can do.

They wished him well. She was to accompany them down the hall a ways.

Harold said what he could to Ms. Brown.

— I'm afraid they don't know how he is doing, she said.

The Unorthodox Ox

— But he's a tough nut and he has a strong constitution, he said.

— He did, but not so much any more, I'm afraid.

She assured them that he had enjoyed their visit. They said goodbye.

Hospital staff was attending to an emergency. Doctors and nurses ran by calling out urgent instructions.

— We might have told him what time it was, he said.

— Look at these people. So there are worse places to work than where we work. They're in a panic, Isa said.

— I don't know, I think what we do is worse. To be contemplating the prospect of wholesale annihilation of life on the planet day in and day out is worse.

— But what we do is not immediate. An immediate situation is always more pressing.

The moaning of a patient's agony coming from a room they passed lent itself to her argument.

— Then she was a teacher and he's a minister. How sweet. I'm glad I came along. I found that touching. Then judging by the way she read to him she has to love him unconditionally.

— Is that ever possible, do you think?

— So Harold, while we're here I would like to visit the maternity ward, since I've been thinking about having a child to unconditionally love. I would like to look at the newborns. I want to see some mothers and their little babies.

— You're interested in being a mother? Are you?

— Who wouldn't be? I've been thinking about it, but I would need a father for the child, and if you could help me out and be pressed into service.

— Help you out?

— You wouldn't say no to me.

— You're asking me to help you?

— You don't have to make up your mind right away, although I will be ready for an answer in exactly three days.

— I'm maybe the wrong person for what you're requesting.

— You would be as good as the next man, and I could trust you to keep a secret.

— Isa, you wouldn't keep the secret yourself.

— I might and I'm always open to bribery. But really I can

promise that you would not be held accountable in any way.

— I am always accountable. Am I not?

They came to the maternity ward. A mother walked by talking to her child that she was cuddling in her arms.

— I'd be grateful, she said.

— I know you would be, so would I probably, and that's what I would be afraid of.

— Look at me. I am as serious as can be.

— I can see that.

He left her at the maternity ward viewing window.

He saw Karol off on her trip.

— I shall miss you, he said to her.

She flew off south.

That evening he received word of the pastor passing on.

So it was documented and undeniably confirmed in the final medical report, that the patient's liver and kidneys had failed. There was nothing that could have been done to have saved him. One last drink would not have mattered.

Then it was by one account, that the minister's last words had been inaudible, and there was only a last groan or grunt to remember or a silently whispered, "Be merciful my Lord."

§

He was sitting on her black couch sipping brandy from a snifter.

— I honestly believe that there shouldn't be anything wrong in having a drink to honour his memory. Then Mary-Adeline, I am thinking that he had told me that he had a sermon that he had written that was addressed to murderers. From what he had said, it was about what motivates people to kill one another. I'd like to read it. And I could get a copy of it from the Diocese, ask his friend the Bishop. I would say to the Bishop. 'I remember he had a sermon on murder that he wanted me to listen to. I'd like to get a copy of it. Sir, you remember I was the man who participated in the final binge with him that resulted in his ultimate demise. I am curious to see if I can be forgiven. I would like to think I would be.' But this isn't right, because I am the one who ought to be forgiving others, and I am the one who should be saying, 'I'm to be forgiven. I forgive myself. I forgive everyone.' But I know I could be held accountable for what's happened because of my ill-will towards organized religion. I am not a noble man. I am a bad person through and through.

— A little wicked, she said.

— But we have no choice but to be contemptible, foul, loathsome, hateful, sinful, corrupt, evil, murderous, and human?

— Maybe not.

— What hope is there if that is true? We can't believe that.

— There is not much to be done about it.

He finished his drink, he poured himself another, and he helped himself to a gianduja with feuilletine coated in dark chocolate.

— Still there is hope, he sighed.

— There is, there is, she said.

— These are delicious. It's the devil's food.

He went home to pack what he needed for their trip north.

Then there was a note at home with instructions for what he was to take care of while Karol was gone. If he were not to do so, he would regret not having done so, he would, she had promised him in her note.

First on the list for what was being asked of him was for him to go and retrieve his shirt that was in the neighbour's yard where he had thrown it. So in talking to the neighbour, he asked the man, if while he was away, if he would look after and see to filling their bird feeder. That was not a problem apparently.

The neighbour already knew that word had it that the minister's funeral was to be for the weekend of the following week.

— You'll be back for his funeral? The neighbour asked him.

— For the following weekend, I will, yes.

— What a codger he was, a lush, but a good guy. Friendly as could be.

— He was.

— Poor old drunken sod.

Harold threw away the shirt.

Some of what else that he was instructed to take care of in the note he looked after.

III

The next morning they left on their trip and they drove away from death, sorrow, and the scandal.

He had wanted to leave the night before. The urge to get away had been weighing on his mind. But for them to have made a long journey so late in the day and to be driving so late at night would have been trying.

— My conscience was up to its tricks and kept me up last night. Then Mary-Adeline, I had to have known he wasn't going to live much longer. But what difference does it make, a few days more or less in the life of someone? So I will put this behind me, and what a day it is to forget our worries.

She said what put him at ease. He responded.

— Not a care in the world.
— I don't know of one.
— I don't either.
— How easy was that?
— We're on the road. It will be clear sailing all the way up.
— It is a perfect day.
— We couldn't ask for better weather. It will cool off a little, the further north we get.

They were driving through the farming regions and into areas of deciduous forests. They drove past towns that were fewer and farther between and the further they went the closer they got to where they were heading and with a few qualms the further they were from what was being left behind. The coniferous forests of the north became endless.

At an observation site by a lake that he had been reminded of from the *Land Migratory Bird Report* they stopped for lunch. There were birds congregating.

Out onto a promontory that went far out into the lake, they

walked to the end of the point. On warm glacially formed rocks they sat down at the water's edge. Swans, geese, and song birds flew in for the crumbs that were to be left behind. A duck formation landed, flying in from him blowing on his duck caller.

Then as they were enjoying their lunch he got on to the topic of what accounts for the enthusiasm that birdwatchers have and for why they will spend many hours out in cold, wet, and windy weather observing the permutations of bird behaviour.

— This is heaven here for an ornithologist. We can come to a spot like this and not move for hours and while away the time amongst our feathered friends. And there's a quality about birds for us to envy, the anatideas, the web-foots, they don't mind being observed. They do nothing to make a secret of their activities, as if to say, 'I'm a duck. I don't care what others think of my foolish behaviour.' Yet they're faithful to each other. Swans and geese mate for life, as do some ducks, the Harlequin Duck, for example, named for being the clown of ducks. He's a faithful clown. We won't see one here. They live near fast-running water or near the ocean.

They finished their lunch and drove on. They drove for several hours. In the late afternoon they arrived.

The property had a lake that was surrounded by an uncut forest that had been growing to its near full height. Tree branches and the fascicles of needles shadowed the ground. There was no underbrush. The cottage was by the water and overlooking the lake. On the north wall was a round stone chimney. There was the fragrance of tree resin that was encompassing.

Then before unpacking the car and going inside the cottage they walked out into the woods and they ran away laughing and springing on a mossy forest floor. They went on and off trails. On lower dead branches they swung from their arms from time to time, and they gave themselves up to making proclamations regarding the creaking expansiveness of the boreal forestation. Then had she wished she could have carried him along with any request she could have made. He would have given in: "I am interested," and there would be silence, a universe of silence before the sound of a baby or a young child crying.

In sunlight that was coming down through the branches they stood where they were for a moment.

— What is it that's always missing? There is always so much of everything, and what's missing? she asked him.

Then there was a gathering of squirrels unused to the slow-moving lethargy of human thought. They were chattering at the interruption to their nut collecting.

— Don't we want to find a clearing when in the woods? she quizzitively asked.

— I don't know of one anywhere close by. We might have to walk for miles.

— Can we?

— It is never too late to walk for miles, he said.

— There's nothing missing, but a small clearing in the woods somewhere and if we don't come to a clearing, we'll know what's missing, she said.

A breeze was blowing through the tree tops. The tree trunks groaned.

— I've a melody from a Mahler symphony in my mind.

She sang it for him.

— How funny Mahler would come to mind now, she said.

They were walking on an ancient animal trail well-trodden by moose, deer, and black bears.

— The wind is whispering, instructing us to: *Follow the trail, go up the hill,* he said.

They walked up a rocky hill.

— *Go past the rock outcrop, the formation, go around it, then go down the hill and if you want, jump into the lake.*

They arrived at the shores of the lake. They took off their clothes. They swam over fish that they could see ten metres below in the clearest of waters.

They got out and they lay on the shore in the setting sun, and they were listening to and interpreting the noises around them of: feeding trout jumping, twittering birds, chattering squirrels, burrowing rodents, buzzing insects, and in that interpretation, the man, the woman, and nature were nearly indivisible.

So it was all throughout the week, if and when they were in the cottage next to the fire, or if out walking in the woods or if they were swimming in the lakes; they were to continue to further adventure into a deepening communion with one another and the

The Unorthodox Ox

area and they were almost or actually reading each other's minds in a way akin to understanding incomprehensible acts of phenomenon.

She had played for him all of the Partitas and Sonatas and other solo works for violin by Bach and an arrangement for violin of the D minor fugue for organ. And the number of times he had wanted to almost fall over backwards from indescribable happiness he lost track of.

And Mary-Adeline had thought of things that she couldn't believe to be anything but wonderfully strange and inexplicable, like the melodies and harmonies of Mahler or an overgrown clearing in the woods. Nothing seemed to be missing. "I would like to go on and on, blindfolded like this," one of them had said to the other.

Then the week was to be remembered but not brought back in accurate recollection as to the pleasures experienced, but this was not to be regretted, since such experiences are the grounding from which regret springs, grows and flourishes, for the old who refuse to let their last enemy take them away.

So on the morning of their departure they took a last long walk in the woods. They avoided the subject of the future.

On the journey back they took their time, stopping for anything and everything that could have afforded a detour and delay them.

When they drove into the farming regions they saw how during the week in the fields the corn had ripened. The harvesting had begun.

At her house they divulged their hopes and voiced concerns. "But now, what? I don't know. What now?"

They sat in her living room wondering about what did not have a perfect solution and they ended up setting up their next rendezvous.

He drove on home.

§

So there was destiny that he would not have believed possible, but it was inevitable, despite his or anyone's incredulity.

It was as it was and seemed that during the recent process of probating his late mother's estate; it had come to light when marshalling investments and in settling the estate, that there were holdings for which he was the beneficiary and there were varied short-term and long-term government and cooperate bonds, equities, private and commercial real estate. A contracted chartered accountant, in completing an inventory and an evaluation of the assets (for what the gains and the liabilities amounted to) had come to determine the worth of what was the portfolio of the holdings. So it had been apparently, that the assets in the portfolio, over decades, had been administered and invested wisely, by an appointed nominee of the long deceased relative to whom the original interests had belonged, and those assets, i.e.; the different investment vehicles, they had been in trust. The trust was open. So it was evident then — how there had been transactions conducted by the nominee, in keeping with the deceased relative's original wishes, he having predicted prior to his death where future investments were to be made. So then it was from the principle amount, that had not been meagre at the time when initially invested, that monies had accrued and exponentially compounded.

A message for him from the accountant asked him to call. What a conversation he had with the accountant.

There was documentation that had been sent to him to read, and those papers he looked over. He carefully studied the figures, breaking down the numbers to see how the value of the money had grown over time. He need not have bothered, as it was obvious enough when he compared the difference of the original principle and the final sum that the ratio for the numbers added up to a respectable amount. But he went through his calculations, and in doing so he appreciated how his outlook was not what it had always been.

He was going to be able to pay his debts: the funeral expenses, the wedding expenses, and the debt to the municipality. There were debts that he could pay off that he would have wanted to leave outstanding to annoy creditors, those he would pay, and it was for the first time in his life that he was maybe going to be magnanimously generous to a fault.

He reread the documents and he marvelled at how the change that was coming was bordering on the miraculous, and to think by another twist, by that time, he may have been worse off, much worse off.

He gathered up unpaid bills. He got out a chequebook and in a flurry he wrote out cheques and apologies for delay of payment, and he put them in envelopes, though he did not do so for the municipal debt. No apology was in order for that.

Then it occurred to him, that he might get some satisfaction in settling up that matter, so he decided that he would pay off Councillor Elrod in person, see after what was a personal reckoning, and take that problem by the horns as it were.

Then he was to get the note with the instructions that Karol had left for him, as for what he had to take care of according to the instructions and he went about the house to prepare for her return. He tidied the place up. He dusted furniture. He took out some rotting garbage that he had forgotten to take out before he had left on his trip. He opened up all the windows in the house. He went outside and he filled the bird feeder that the neighbour had neglected to look after. Oh well. He saw to whatever else there was to do.

Then with the envelope with the cheque in it he went off to the Councillor's to settle the score.

He was going along the street and he ran into no one that he had to stop and speak to and there was no one he knew who would have recognized the generous man that he was to become. But it was when he was walking by in front of a house that had a "Beware of Dog" warning sign, that a mad dog came rushing out. The animal charged him, barking, growling, and snarling at him viciously. But the enraged beast he ignored, such was his purpose. The dog nipped at him several times, backed off, sat down, and it wagged its tail as if they were to become friends for life and he was the new master.

Then the dog watched him to see where he was going and to wait for him to return, and so to find out who was whose best friend.

Councillor Elrod was standing out at the end of his driveway. He was by his mailbox, hunched over it. There were tools on the ground that he had to have been making use of.

— It's a bad time, Councillor? Forgive me if it is.

— No, I'm just repairing my mailbox. I'm having trouble getting the flag on it to stay up.

He raised the flag on the mailbox and let it go. It fell.

— That can be a problem, not being able to keep one's flag up, Councillor.

— It's nothing too serious.

— It's convenient you're here as I've come to deliver a cheque to you. I have.

He handed him the envelope.

— Check for yourself to be sure we understand each other, because I would like to see you are satisfied and that I am satisfied. It is for the full amount you will see.

The Councillor agreed that he would be pleased if that were the case. He nodded with peculiar emphasis, indicating how he would like to see for himself if they had come to an agreement. He speared a screwdriver into the ground. He got out a pocket-knife, unfolded the blade, routinely rubbed his thumb over the edge of it. He opened an end of the envelope with the knife, took out the cheque, verified the amount, closed his knife and pocketed it, put the cheque back in the envelope, and he raised his eyebrows several times, signalling the degree of satisfaction that he would not have expected to experience so thoroughly. The conversation had stopped during the deliberations.

— You decided not to take the legal route, said the Councillor.

— It wasn't worth it.

— A wise decision.

— I saw what was what.

— It's for the best.

— Then I should like to take this opportunity to thank you again for the work done on the Plover site.

— You're welcome. We're still hoping we'll catch the delinquents who were responsible.

— You will get them to pay for it no doubt.

— Our laws are to be upheld. It's incumbent on us to uphold the law.

— I'm of that conviction, too.

— And might I ask if you are going to the minister's funeral tomorrow?

— I am, of course.

— I am, as well. So I've heard that people are divided into two camps about what occurred. I haven't taken sides on it.

— The loss of his church was hard on him, Councillor. It hit him hard. In fact, I am pretty sure that it must have killed him.

— I hope not. Anyway, I thank you for the payment.

The Unorthodox Ox

— Then good luck with your elections, Elrod.

— I thank you and I can't expect you to vote for me, I suppose.

— No, I'll vote for you, because you know how to get the job done. Few people in your position do, know how to do that, are able to or even give a damn.

— I am always glad to do what I can. So I should get back to this.

He lifted up the flag.

— Keep it up, Elrod.

The flag fell.

— It was squeaking. I greased the joint too much. I don't know how I am going to fix it to be honest.

That they hopefully would not have to meet too often, for that, they shook hands.

He met no one going back.

He drove to pick Karol up.

§

— So you would like me to believe, Harold, you want me to believe, that I should not have been worried about you, that I wouldn't have been. How could you have thought that? What were you thinking? Karol asked him when they were in his car.

— You weren't worried about me, Karol.

— I called your assistant. She told me you would call me. Then she didn't tell me where you were. She said you were out and that you would call. I spoke to her several times.

— She's loyal to me and she would not have revealed my whereabouts.

— I don't get it.

— We were going to see each other soon enough.

— I don't know what this means.

— You know what it means.

— I don't.

— You might.

— No.

— You do.

— You've taken leave of your senses.

— I have come to my senses.

From off the back of a truck in front of them that was hauling a harvested load chaff was rising up and raining down onto the windshield.

So he happened to notice that she was beside herself from anger, and she did not appear to know what to say and seemed unable to speak. He seized the moment.

— And Karol, you should be advised maybe that at George's funeral tomorrow that it's likely that you'll have to answer what will be awkward questions. Someone will ask you. 'How does your husband feel about his part in it?' Is the sort of question you might have to answer. I'd suggest your response to that would be to say it hasn't been easy for me, and if you want to believe it you can think that I had to get away from the outcry surrounding the circumstances of his death to let things settle down a little.

She let out a cry of fury that ought to have given him a moment's pause. He continued.

— Also there's something else you'll be interested for me to tell you. I've paid off the settlement money to the municipality. The case would have been next to impossible to win. It would have taken a lot of money and time to fight. Now we don't have to worry about it.

—What did you do?

— I've paid it off, all of it.

— What are you saying? You couldn't have paid it.

— I wouldn't say I did if I didn't.

— That's what you did?

— There is money coming in from the estate settlement. It's a substantial amount of money, more than expected.

— Is there? How much? How much money?

— It's a respectable sum.

— Is it?

— It's a surprising amount.

— You won't tell me how much?

— I don't think I will, tell you how much. I'd rather not for some reason.

— You decided to pay it! Did you?!

— We'd have had to pay more than the original amount owed with the interest and penalties if we lost. You've no idea how much more. There's no question in anyone's mind we would have lost. I

used the emergency fund to temporarily pay it off until the settlement comes in.
— How much more would we have had to pay, Harold?
— You've no idea.
— I have no idea?
— You don't.
— You're sure about that?
— As can be.
— I'm not.
— I am.
— No, you're not.
— I am.
— You've lost your goddamn mind!
— You lost yours, I lost mine, when? The day we met? The day we became friendly? We both lost it.

She interrupted him. He interrupted her in return.

— But why did I come back that last time? Why? Because my time should have been up. So was our time up a long time ago? Then you know something happened before George died. There was significant meaning to it. He didn't know what time it was before he died. His watch had been taken from him. He didn't know the time. So he died wanting to know if his time was up? And I'm wondering if he had had his watch would he have looked at it and said to himself or anyone else, 'Christ Almighty, screw this life of mine, it is now my time. I can go in peace.'

— What are you talking about?

— You've never known what I've been talking about. Even now you don't know.

They arrived home. She asked for him to leave her alone. She took her bags into the house.

He then went into the garage and he got an axe, and he turned on the floodlight for the yard, then into the surface of her tree stump he wedged the axe in the same moment when she was looking out a window that she was closing. She howled at him.

— You left every window in the house open, and what are you doing now?

— I'm going to chop some wood and work off some steam is what I'm doing.

He pulled the axe from the stump and re-wedged it with all the liberating force he had within himself.

— I'm going to chop some wood, as you had instructed in your note. Then you know what Karol, you must forgive me if by chance I ever led you to believe I was predictable. I'm not. No. And really the truth of it is, is that one lie will cause infinite distrust. That's all it takes, one lie. One thread of doubt and the fabric of truth unravels and we are naked before it. So much for appearances.

She slammed a window. She slammed all the windows.

Then he got the wood he was going to cut up and chopped it into kindling until exhausted, and instead of piling it up for the winter, he might have burned it, there and then, as he was not going to be around to stay warm from the work he had lathered himself into a heated sweat over on that cool night.

He went to Mary-Adeline's. He did not return to his previous home that night.

The next morning the two of them accompanied each other to the minister's funeral.

§

It was one minister after another, his colleagues, they spoke about salvation and paradise: the final reward for a lifetime of devotion and worship, the themes of the profession. But none of the men provided personal testimony about their friend that they were there to memorialize.

The burial was similarly unmemorable for what was said, due to the diminutive presence and failing voice of the one old minister who performed the final tribute, and there were occasional words, stifled crying and other mumblings of ministers heard.

He had received a message from Karol telling him that she was not going to attend the funeral nor the burial. She was at her mother's. In her absence Harold had gone home to get his mourning attire.

Mary-Adeline was dressed elegantly as if for a performance.

They were standing at a distance off from the main group that was crowding around the open grave.

"Amen" and mumbling.

The Unorthodox Ox

— This is an unimpressive showing is what this is. It's dismal. We might ask if they're trying to do their best and if they are, what can we do? We could walk off to show our disapproval. But I can't. No, I can't, if I can help it. Stop me Mary-Adeline if you see me trying to sneak away when no one is looking. God, I feel guilty all of the sudden. I didn't even feel this guilty when my mother passed away.

— You would leave me here? she asked.

— No, we could run off together, and to be seen to be leaving arm in arm and this being our first public appearance. It would confirm the rumours about us.

"Amen."

— That would not be as amazing as the truth only hearsay.

"Amen."

Trudi Brown was also standing off by herself, holding onto her agony. He acknowledged her.

— Poor Ms. Brown, she should be the one to be speaking on his behalf. So I hope it will never happen that those we care for will mourn for those they cherish, but it will.

The unmarried widow was struggling to not outwardly express her inward feelings of unimaginable sadness.

— Trudi, was a gifted math teacher. I remember she said to me once that the greatest conclusion a mathematician can come to is when he or she has nothing. Would she say that now? Is it not a romantic idea? A mathematical, yet a romantic idea.

She agreed and quietly, almost inaudibly, she was humming a tune he thought he knew the name of. He accompanied her humming with his thoughts that he shared with her.

— I like cemeteries, the sombreness in the air, the sense of timelessness in the lives of those at rest, the loss we are reminded of, the skeleton look of cypress trees, the loneliness and dread on the faces of those who are afraid to consider what has happened, is happening, and will happen to themselves.

Mourners looked at him. He nodded back.

— Tonight everyone here will look into a mirror and ask themselves a few questions.

The ceremony ended. People separated into smaller groups that went off into the surrounding monuments. They were engaging in supportive conversations.

Trudi Brown moved off to keep her distance.

Then he and Mary-Adeline were to be the first to offer her their kindness. He said to Ms. Brown what was consoling.

— That you were at his side at the end had to have reassured him, Trudi, said Harold.

— Well, I want to believe he's all right now. I'd like to think he is, she said.

A rook landed in a nearby tree.

— But I am not too sure if I was of much comfort to him. He was to me though. Then now I'm thinking of going back to Ireland. So at home we know how to send a person off. Did anyone understand what those men were saying? I didn't make sense out of it at all. And priests and ministers don't know how to communicate any more. It didn't used to be like that. They used to know what to say and when, that much they were able to do. They were his friends those old men? I never knew any of his friends. How would he have introduced me?

Then out from a group Helen came along towards them.

— Trudi, I would like to pay my respects, if I may, she said.

— You are sorry for my troubles, thank you, Helen. That is kind of you.

— He was a noble man.

— He'd be pleased to hear us say so.

— He was a guiding spirit to many of us.

— When he wasn't making a holy show of himself he was that.

— He was good at his vocation. He will be missed. He helped out a lot of people with his acts of generosity. We are sorry for his loss.

— We are.

— Then Trudi, you know, you and I, we are not getting any younger and our time will come, too. Think of only yesterday, we were young and look at us, old as the hills, two old crones. But we have our health, and we have to stay healthy as long as we can.

Several rooks flew by and over.

— We have to take care of ourselves, and we don't want to drink too much, said Helen.

They laughed.

— We might live to be a hundred if we have to.

The Unorthodox Ox

— I hope not, said Trudi.

— I am hoping not either. It won't be so long as that.

They looked for another topic for discussion, but they were at a loss. They were at a sad loss.

Then the retired bereaved teacher excused herself. She walked towards the grave. At its edge she looked down into it. She threw flowers onto the lid of the casket and she wept.

— That love affair they had was one-sided for both of them. So she's on her own now, said Helen to her son-in-law and to his mistress.

But she changed the subject then and she said to Mary-Adeline that she recalled how they had spoken briefly at the church demolition, and that at that time she had wanted to say to her that she had enjoyed listening to a recording of hers, and she had been hoping to get other recordings and what might she recommend? She was wondering if she could recommend anything in particular, yet she liked to listen to anything, really, she said.

Harold suggested to her that what she would like would entirely depend on the kind of music that she liked more than others.

— But you know me, Harold. Sometimes I don't know what I like or want or I can't make up my mind, and you know what that is like.

— I can recommend the Bach recordings, he said.

— There is an available set of the concertos, said Mary-Adeline.

— I shall look for them then.

— They are in the catalogue.

— Then I read you tour a lot which must be exciting, said Helen.

— I travel more than I'd like to, yes, said Mary-Adeline.

— It must be quite exciting. Then it is an honour to have you living here in our town.

From the graveside was a cry of anguish.

— That poor woman, he was all she had that we know of. Some say she got what she deserved, but that's not kind to even think that. I shouldn't repeat it. Well, I must go. I don't want to hang around here too long, lot's of time for that when I'm ready.

— I will wait for her and accompany her, he said.

— Tell her. Oh, I don't know what else to say. Didn't I already say enough, maybe too much? I think I did. I shall look for those recordings. Bye, bye.

She joined a group of mourners who were heading towards the cemetery gates.

— She knew I didn't go home last night, which means she was being discreet. I think she was being devious by being so discreet. What a wily woman she is.

Trudi Brown was wailing. She stepped back away from the grave and walked off a ways. She leaned against a nearby monument and she was sobbing.

— There is nothing that we can do for her? Mary-Adeline asked.

— Not that I know of.

Ms. Brown shouted.

— Why have you left me, George? Why do I have to go on living without you?

She walked back to the grave and looked down into it. She was crying more softly.

— But it is a waste of an opportunity for happiness to be squandered, and there are love affairs that are not only one-sided, he said.

— There are, she said.

— They shouldn't be allowed to be squandered. It's tragic when that happens.

The ex-teacher who had taught thousands of students in her day was exhausting what she had called on to relieve her untold grief.

So the day's events were winding down. An old chapter in the lives of some was coming to its end, a new one was beginning for others.

Then it was not far off to one side of the cemetery, there was the sound of a motor, a dirt excavator starting up, and the engine got louder as it was coming towards them up the lanes, down one, the next, it turned at their side-road. The machine pulled up before the grave. The operator turned the motor off. It coughed several times and painfully died.

The gravedigger gestured to them and asked to excuse himself, and he explained the reason for disturbing them. There were burials for the following day. He was doing his job. He begged their pardon a second time.

Trudi Brown did not appear to understand what was about to happen, but she moved away from the grave nevertheless.

The Unorthodox Ox

Harold waved to the man for mercy's sake to get on with it. The gravedigger started the motor up, it roared louder than they would have wanted.

He called out over the howling engine.

— Mary-Adeline, what a day for us!

— What?

She could not hear him.

— I am happy, he screamed louder.

— Did you say you're happy? So am I!

— I'm happy! Yes!

— Me too!

— I couldn't be happier if this was the happiest day of my life.

The grave was filled. The man waved and drove off.

In the dirt of the mound were small stones. Trudi Brown picked them out and threw them away. They helped her. Dirt without stones in it remained when they finished.

— He'll be all right one way or another. I don't know what they will put on his marker. I'd have suggested: *May the grass grow long on the road to hell for want of use*. That would be fitting, she said.

They walked with her to the cemetery gates. They spoke their last condolences.

She got on her bicycle and she disappeared.

Then it was some time later that Ms. Trudi Brown was to be remembered by those who had known her and would remember her fondly and she would be remembered by some who would remember from her teachings that an Isosceles Triangle had two equal sides and the Pythagorean theorem illustrated this fact, as does life. They watched her set out and ride off.

— She came on a bicycle. What a funny race are the Irish, he said.

The gravedigger was working on another hole.

— If someone were to say about someone who's now dead that they'd be better off alive? he asked.

— It would be a nice thing to say, you're right, she said.

— Shall we go somewhere else? That machine is a grim reminder of so much that is wrong with the world.

They went to another location where there they said what they both wanted to hear. Now and forever, yes, yes, they were happy.

The sun was setting and there was above and below blankets of thinly layered clouds light coming out from under them and keeping the evening sky alive for a few more moments.

Mary-Adeline drove him back to his car that he had left at the cemetery.

§

Goodbye once and for all.

— We should hope there's not a reason for us to begrudge one another for too long, he said to Karol.

He was deciding what he would have to come back to pick up at another time.

— That's everything you're going to take for now? Karol asked him.

— For now.

She gave him that morning's *Frogwatch Observation Form*. She told him that she would continue participating.

— Apart from everything, he trailed off with the idea.

— Harold, it is not as if you are going to actually sum everything up in a few words.

— I am not good at that.

— You better go now.

— Let us think well of each other maybe.

— Sure.

— Why not?

She stood at the door to watch him go.

— Bye.

She walked to the back of the house and she went out into the backyard and she was looking out into the field, and she was giving up on him having a change of heart and of him returning and begging for her forgiveness.

Later, it was amongst her papers, drawings and pictures, she found a note he had written for her. It said: *I wish you the best, goodbye.* That he had not intended to necessarily wait for her to return before he left saddened her.

The Unorthodox Ox

§

If an arbitrary man was able to reconcile inconsistencies in different versions of what is a familiar story as it unfolded, maybe, perhaps, he might or would investigate if there are inaccuracies, misrepresentations, false interpretations, if and when being invited to operate as the removed third eye and he is an agent on a mission, an agent within a story, inside the story, but not knowing to whom it relates to specifically, necessarily, but still, to be of the western world, to be linked to Greek, Roman, Jewish, Muslim, and Christian mythologies, to be a victim of brutal systems that are unimaginably inhuman. Well, needless to say, that would be a considerable amount of complication to wade through and come to lasting terms with.

But such speculation he was to ignore, as for what was "what" and "why" "how" or "anything", as on that day, she and he, that day, they were to celebrate the day and hope and expect what was to come. Mary-Adeline and Harold were to celebrate and spare no pains in doing so to mark the occasion.

They were to spend that first night that was a night that was to be the beginning of what was to be the rest of their long lives. They were to spend that night together in luxurious comfort in a high-end luxury hotel, in the bridal suite.

He had made the arrangements and before she was to arrive, he checked up on and was to look after, what were the amenities, to be sure the suite was as it had to be and that there would not have been a reason for them to complain.

The hotel was a landmark and a heritage site protected against the future. The penthouse suite was the complete top floor. It had a full and open view of the horizon that in contemplation a happily married man and woman would have yearned to look towards but not too far beyond.

The rooms were contemporarily furnished and decorated, and during the showing and later on his own private inspection he picked up on how much care had been afforded and that there was much more than what are average comforts on offer. He emphasized particularly in his mind's eye the size of the bath, for the voluminous amount of water it had to have held. Four hundred and sixty-two litres he calculated at a glance. He noted the texture of the Kashmir draperies, soft and velvety to one's touch. There were hand sewn custom-made vintage lampshades. Woven rugs were thrown where one was likely to tread barefoot early in the chilliness of the morning. Fresh flowers were in vases and their fragrance was different in each room. The king-size bed might have bedded down large families. He was pleased and he admired the suite that he already might have spent a night in, in a memorable dream that he had always wanted to have.

He was grateful as he was wandering around in such opulence. He was tempted to fill the bath and have it ready and steaming for Mary-Adeline's arrival, but it was too early for such silliness.

He was walking around through the rooms padding over the carpets. Then he sat down in a throne like chair to make himself as comfortable as could be, and after some time he was in fact relaxed.

But it was not before too long that he had the idea of speaking with someone who was a long-time friend. He was a man in a situation similar to his own, who had left his wife.

So it was to be helpful to share his news with a friend, who would have had to have understood, and to talk about what he had to look forward to. He called his friend.

What had happened before, during, and afterwards, and that he was in a hotel and why he was there, he related.

— I'm on top of the world and it's downhill from here, I tell you.

— Congratulations.

— I am out from under a yoke.

— That's great and don't let it bother you if I envy you. You realize you're gloating to someone who doesn't have visiting rights to see his children. But some are lucky and others of us are cursed from the day we were born.

— There is no going back this time, Harold laughed.

— You've misgivings?

— I've always wanted to be honourable.

— Forget it. Look what good it did for me being honourable.

— You have been unlucky.

— Hold on, I offer you my support and you're mocking me.

— I'm talking about hope.

— You're being insensitive, Harold.

— I can't help myself. I am so excited.

— You're the lucky one.
— It means a lot that you are telling me that.
They wished for each other the best of luck.
Mary-Adeline arrived.

They ate the evening meal out on the rooftop terrace. They watched the sun fall before their eyes. The food was sumptuous. They sipped chilled champagne. They asked what the other was thinking, and when they finished the meal they sat in silence, in a perfect still silence, knowing more or less what the other was thinking.

Then in the unseasonably warm autumn night they went out for a walk. They walked along the shore of a shoreline path around a lake. Mist was rising on the water, and they were in a fog that was swirling and she put it to him. Who was better off than they were to not be lost in the fog? He knew of no one. The hotel had been a nice touch. She complimented him for it. They returned to the suite.

Then at one point when delirious with joy he opened up the suitcase he had brought, and they threw the contents of it willy-nilly around the room. He then filled the bath.

§

Isa Martin de Aguilera questioned him. She cross-examined him.
— I can't grasp why you would have taken on a mistress, she neddled him.
— To love someone. There shouldn't be anything wrong with that necessarily.
— How long has it been going on for? Christ Almighty!
— I had a reason not to mention it, not too long.
— Why's that?
— I wanted to see how things would turn out.
— I'm bowled over. I'm floored.
— Then for some time I've been working for the money and no other reason. Now I don't need it. I'm rather well-off.
— But Harold you can't leave me. I forbid this. This is terrible news. I am not happy for you at all.
— You know I was going to take the first chance that came along and run for my life. I don't think I could stay on and be so

ineffectual as I have been. What good is that for anyone?

— But it has been you and me slaving away. It has been as if it were you and me keeping things together.

— Yes, we have tried.

— You're serious? You are dead serious then.

— If it made you feel better, I wish I could say I wasn't.

— What are you going to do with yourself now?

— We will be travelling. It's nice to travel when in love.

— That can be a nightmare.

— It won't be. We had a good time up north.

— Then who do I save now?

— Yourself.

— Who will save you?

— She will, already has.

— You think it's love? You think you are in love with whoever she is? Does she love you in return? It hasn't been for too long, you said.

— I think so, there's no other way to describe it that I am aware of. But Isa, don't worry, there will be someone to replace me, and there are billions of us out there waiting to do what I would have liked to have done but have not succeeded at.

— But I was hoping that you were going to willingly volunteer to father a child for me. I was serious.

— I hadn't forgotten.

— I wasn't going to let you forget. So what was the problem, our problem?

— Timing, timing was it.

— Who is she?

— You might have heard of her.

He told her who Mary-Adeline was and what in a short time she had come to mean to him.

— I know I ought to be pleased for you, but maybe it won't work out, and you will come crawling back to get your job back.

— Then Isa, I shall have to pick out a letter of resignation. Imagine that, after all these years.

They laughed in concert.

She then told him he would have to remember her from a moment when they had been having a good time.

The Unorthodox Ox

— In a week you won't miss me, he said sympathetically.
— When the shock passes I'll be furious at you. How can you leave me? How can you abandon me?
— And would you like to pick out a resignation letter for me?
— No, I don't think I'm going to pick out a letter for you.
— I knew you wouldn't. But I had to ask, so that you wouldn't have asked me why I hadn't asked.
— No, no.
— I'll make sure there is nothing in it that can be traced back to you. I will be careful.
— I wouldn't have thought of that.
— We can never be too careful.
— Be careful then. You need to be careful, it sounds like.

§

Then when looking through the file of his letters of resignation, he did not find one that was right for its purpose. None of the letters were appropriate.

So he had to write an updated letter, and drawing on information from several of the letters, he composed his final letter of resignation.

Then it was the second-to-last-draft, out of four drafts, that was the version that found itself to be on file permanently.

Letter of resignation—draft #3.

Dear Colleagues:

I am informing you of my resignation that is to take place effective immediately. Please forgive the precipitousness of this decision that would be complicated to explain. However, nevertheless, to offer a measure of justification for my departure I would like to voice concerns for some issues that I have had for some time.

(A section was missing in the third draft.)

So in conclusion, when having to evaluate our programs: The Land Migratory Bird Studies, The Fish Hatching Project, The Frogwatch Program, The Genetic Modification Studies, The Backyard Bird Count, The Seedling Surveys, *and* The Sixth Mass Extinction, *we have to concede that these programs are flawed and they have been left open-ended and will continue on for many years* (words missing)... *And now, the actual connection between the results of our studies and the measures taken to make the results meaningful were not in the process of their realization elaborated on in a manner as to allow the results to be altogether applicably conceived. Take for example the C-5 law that we spent so much time on. For that, we underestimated possibilities and limitations. We overlooked a number of unforeseen occurrences, despite calculated odds that weighed irrefutably on the side of larger numbers. This because our methodology assumes too much, but does not assume assumptions are being made. Then when one thinks of the number of times that we approved of what we had been assigned to do, knowing full well that the assignment was problematic. However, we proceeded. So we have monitored: migrating birds, frogs, fish, beetle reproduction, subtle evolutionary changes, the number of seedlings that survived. But will it happen that some day there will be nothing too remote or insignificant for us to investigate and impose theories onto? But why is it we do not ask "why"? Why is the "why" not important? Do we know? But if we don't know. Then how can we know enough to ask even that, if we don't even know that? Or is that the problem? And maybe because I have been unable to follow an exact line of inquiry, it is for this if maybe not for other reasons that I am tendering my resignation that I am offering in thanks for the opportunity to reach such a conclusion.*

Sincerely,
Harold T.

Then he filled out an employee evaluation form for himself, it was his own evaluation to send along with his resignation letter. Though his self-evaluation was not important and he was only to have evaluated himself because he had to complete more importantly evaluations for his *people*. That was the final task for him to complete, and so he had thought that he would practise on himself before then evaluating others. Then for his own self-worth, he had been complimentary and not honestly critical, but not so for those whose jobs were on the line.

And it was as he was working through the dismissal confirmation papers, the forms that he had worked on before, that he had to approve by signing, that he found included a request that was for his assistant to be summarily dismissed. He had not known that there was a case against her, but it did not surprise him, as there were those who had it against her for being the one to pass along his critical comments.

However, the case against her was unjustifiable. It rested on unverifiable evidence, it was based on false allegations. It was mean-spirited in intent, an exercise in character assassination.

He might not have signed her dismissal papers; he could have passed them on to the person who was to follow after him or he ought to have drafted a letter in her defence and asked for a review that likely would have led to deciding in her favour. But his decision to have her go when he was leaving he believed he could justify. So he concluded that he was rendering her a service by anticipating the inevitable on her behalf.

He wrote a letter of thanks for her services.

Word got out that he was leaving and as expected, as was the custom, his colleagues organized a farewell party. Then it was later in the day. A group gathered together to wish him well and hope the best for him.

Of course, there were those who were surprised and suspicious regarding his departure. They could not have imagined what his reasons for leaving were. He maintained that it was personal and that he had not committed indiscretions. Then there were a few of his closer associates who asked him how his departure might affect them directly. He was not inclined to let on what he knew for what they would find out when they received their evaluations or dismissals.

But there was the case of the intern, Miss Llewellyn, to whom he thought it would have been interesting to speak to and so to explain what a recommendation might mean for a person who was beginning her career and for someone who had a promising future. Also as she was a new arrival he was perhaps hoping that she, like Isa, would have been someone else who would speak well of him when he was gone, and that might have preserved his memory in some way, but he had no doubt for how it would quickly fade away in the future and into the past.

He invited for Miss Llewellyn, if she would, to take a seat across from him in his office.

— You'll find yourself in my position one day, Miss Llewellyn, maybe seated where I am, and to have been responsible for so much but able to have accomplished so little. It could happen. But you needn't worry why I've called you: to explain how we evaluate ourselves, if and when we ask if we have failed and who's to blame if we have? Or can we cast blame elsewhere? But we prefer to ask others about their failings rather than question our own. You wouldn't venture to say otherwise probably. Neither would I, except in a moment of weakness. Now may be such a moment. Then if you'd like to, maybe you would be interested to tell me about what you might say about your time here. Especially since we had discussed matters when I briefed you on your arrival. Say what you want, if you like. I'm out the door. You can tell me what you have heard from others, and if there is anything that I would want to know that I have never had the chance to find out, anything you have heard that I would be interested in, even coming from an unreliable or unknown source, as to what it is that people have thought about one another or about the man for whom they have worked. I've always wanted to know what people were whispering behind my back.

She maintained that she couldn't think of anything, although appeared to be suggesting otherwise. He asked for her own thoughts. So she commented then on what she thought he was asking, but qualified her comments as being her impressions.

— You are not sure, he said.

She seemed still to be suggesting otherwise.

— Yes sir.

— But anyway, I hope I am right in recommending you, and I wish you luck in your career.

Then he thought to mention to her that he was going to include what he had heard from others in her employee evaluation, even though she wasn't to reveal what she might have known. She could thank him for that, but he was not serious.

— There's no need to thank me that I can think of, few ever have.

— But I could say something that could be my evaluation of you, sir?

— Yes?

— If I may, she emphasized.

— By all means. Please.

The Unorthodox Ox

It was obvious that she had known for some time what she was going to say, and she told him that she felt a curious attraction for him. She asked if he had noticed. Then she had been hoping that that was why he had wanted to speak with her, and if he were interested. She would be grateful for his attentions, she said.

Undoubtedly she had anticipated a different response from him.

— I'm sorry. Excuse me, I'm terribly sorry, forgive me, I'm not usually this forward, she said in her defence.

— I doubt that's true, Miss Llewellyn.

— Forgive me if I've caused you embarrassment. I am embarrassed myself.

— There is no need to be, because I don't think there is a man alive who should take embarrassment too seriously.

— I know you are a married man.

— But what is marriage? But a prison that we want to break out of.

— I wanted to ask is all.

— You're correct in thinking that it is better to assume you might be right than to find out you are wrong later when it's too late.

— I am wrong?

— Never assume either way to make a safe bet. You did the right thing.

His voice communicated to her that he was saying, "That it was impossible."

— I had to ask. I like to experiment when I can, she said.

— You are a scientist. The impulse is a natural one to want to experiment.

She was looking at him from out of the corner of both eyes. He couldn't help but encourage her a little.

— I see you are one of those individuals who deserves what she can ask for and get it no matter what. But in this instance I might suggest that you be careful, if and when, assuming someone is who they are or may not even be.

— I know what you mean, which is what I find to be so intriguing, that not knowing and I'd like to know more, if I could, if possible.

— Of course.

— There's only one way to find out more, as I see it, Harold.

May I call you Harold?
— Not only one. It would be preferable if you didn't call me by my name.
— I'm interested in the one way, she insisted dramatically.
— It is interesting. You're right.
— Isn't it? she tossed her head back. She combed out her hair with her fingers.
He wished her well.
Then she had the assurance to ask him for a signed copy of his evaluation. Then perhaps he was impressed by her lack of discretion, and so he would send her an original signed copy. That was as much as he had to offer her. She would cherish it, she said. He shooed her out of his office, and he instructed her not to come back or he would have to fire her. She dared him to and off she went.
He packed his things and made his final arrangements.
Then it was late in the day, he and Isa went over his letter of resignation and she thought that what he had said in his letter was what they believed. She praised how he had hit the mark.
— I will forgive you for what you're doing eventually, she said.
— You will.
They went over reminiscences as they said goodbye and that warmed up for them feelings and stirred up their memories.
He had been able to enjoy himself at the end of his last day, in his last moments in his office, in the final encounters with those he had worked with, in the last thoughts to do with the irritations he had suffered from that had troubled him and might have caused him to take leave of his senses.
— Goodbye, good luck, best of wishes to all.
He was out the door.
But there was a final run that he wanted to make, that was to be a personal taking into account of things to consider for what it was that he had been doing over those many years, and so he set out to drive around to visit his research sites, the projects he had worked on. He went from one to the next, confirming what he knew of his discouraging disappointments, except for the one exception, where out growing in long fields there were rows of pine-trees that testified to the success of the seedlings he had surveyed.
There were untouched natural areas that he drove by that one

day were to be developed into suburbs, towns, and cities.

He called Mary-Adeline to tell her he was soon to be arriving. She was expecting him for a meal that she was preparing. But the signal was lost just as he was to tell her that he was going to make a quick stop at a town that he had never thought of visiting before, always having passed it by. It was to be the last stop on his way he would have told her.

It was an abandoned and uninhabited town in ruin, its streets were overgrown with bushes and trees. The houses had collapsed. The one remaining standing structure was the church.

He was walking about in the ruins and through undergrowth, and to make the pilgrimage he was on he climbed up a mound of a hill to get to the church. He went inside through what was the missing front door.

Out broken windows birds flew out. Some returned to sit in the window openings, perching, waiting for him to go. On a rotting floor he walked around circling for a while until convinced that what had been left of any relics had been made off with and that what they had stood for no longer had value. Through holes and cracks in the ceiling rays of sunlight were shining down. He stood in the light and was warming himself. He remained there a while, losing track of time and what the passing of it meant to one's life. He checked his watch and waited a little longer. Birds kept flying off and returned. This is what occurred as he stood looking up through the broken church roof into the bright white light. But it was as he was ready to leave and as he was stepping out the front door that a red fox or a gray fox, a vixen, ran past him and inside and she disappeared down into a hole in the ground into her den beneath where the altar would have been. This occurrence turned out to be curious if not more so.

He drove on to his new home.

§

They were eating supper in dim flickering candle light.

— The unexpected announcement of my departure surprised my colleagues. Still they organized a sending-off for me. Then I had signed off on firing some of them and I let my faithful assistant go, who toasted me at my farewell party, not suspecting that I had been unwilling to defend her so she could keep her job. So a friend felt betrayed for reasons that are hard to explain. An intern, to whom I gave a recommendation, made a pass at me. Such flattery is likely before a recommendation, not afterwards. I told her I was an unhappily married man and that I had a mistress.

— I'm glad you weren't happily married when we got to know one other.

— I was only happy afterwards, only afterwards. The food is delicious.

He complimented her for the meal.

— So I guess I didn't know what I was thinking about while I was driving around to take stock of what I've been doing for so many years. I stopped in that town for no reason really.

It was from the kitchen, coming into the shadows of the candle light. The uninvited point of view came into view.

— *Asking to be spared?*

— *What?*

— *From what. I'm telling you what is what.*

— I saw a red fox and it walked into the light. Then I saw it was a gray fox. The gray fox is smaller than the red. I should have noticed the difference, unless it happened to be a larger than normal gray fox, but I hadn't immediately noticed the difference between the two. I was confused.

— *Grasping at straws, and there is nothing else to reach for. Really?*

— *What?*

— *Spared from what? Who cares?*

It was to write the day's grocery list and to remind himself to eat, that back into the kitchen he slithered, sliding the door closed.

In the succeeding moments, they considered the implications of what had appeared before them in its unlikeliness.

So it was sometime later then, when they found a grocery list that listed: peaches, apples, cantaloupes, pomegranates, figs, date palms, blueberries, tomatoes, aubergines, Hubbard squash, shrimp, oysters, mussels, lobsters, and other species of shell fish that in the scheme of things might be conceived to be the deep-sea equivalent of beetles.

The Unorthodox Ox

The dessert she had concocted from her fruit trees was delicious.

They were to go over the plans for her tour: the countries, the cities, and the dates for her performances.

The candles were burning down and went out. They were in the dark and they perceived.

§

So it was a paradigm shift of incommensurable possibilities within a dimension that was approaching what was not reality and then to be in a parallel sphere and to survive within a paradox, but not be torn to bits by the contradiction of it. To be in and of a herd and herding animals at the same time (oxen being the animal of preference), and to get to that state will happen when a beast of burden and his master have tamed each other, which is when a man and his ox achieve an understanding while they are toiling and this keeps the master and his beast alive and they rely on one another. Or so it is from the point of view of a principle concept under which smaller concordant concepts mosey along in a symbiotic, synergetic, dynamic relationship of evolving principles, which are not available for popular consumption, as is obvious from an examination of what comes out from the altars of modern prophets, who in their respected fields of expertise are not well-versed in how to interpret their own unadulterated divinations and so do not realize, that the art and science of prophecies is not a science and a lot less an art.

But it is the training, the rigorous and hard discipline: to be whipped relentlessly and have desire mercifully beaten out of one into submission, as happens in moral tales and in parables and is understood in context, if it is the right one, and if the story is the right story and the pictures are recognizably figurative, the words to the point, then there is no room for confusion, given that is the desired effect.

It had been for years, decades perhaps, that there was a cartoon of a man in the company of his domesticated companion, a story in pictures, that in the following series (in order) had been hanging on the walls at *Chez Henri Lai.*

The Unorthodox Ox

Oxherding

1. Undisciplined

With his horns projected in the air the beast snorts,
madly running over the mountain paths, farther and farther
he goes astray!

A dark cloud is spread across the entrance of the valley, who
knows how much of the fine fresh herb is trampled under his
wild hoofs!

2. Discipline Begun

I am in possession of a straw rope, and I pass it through his nose,

For once he makes a frantic attempt to run away, but he is severely whipped and whipped;

The beast resists the training with all the power there is in a nature wild and ungoverned, but the oxherder never relaxes his pulling tether and ever-ready whip.

3. In Harness

Gradually getting into harness the beast is now content to be led by the nose,

Crossing the stream, walking along the mountain path, he follows every step of the leader;

The leader holds the rope tightly in his hand never letting it go. All day long he is on the alert almost unconscious of what fatigue is.

4. Faced Round

After long days of training the result begins to tell and the beast is faced round,

A nature so wild and ungoverned is finally broken, he has become gentler;

But the tender has not yet given him his full confidence,
He still keeps his straw rope with which the ox is now tied to a tree.

5. Tamed

Under the green willow tree and by the ancient mountain stream,

The ox is set at liberty to pursue his own pleasures;

At the eventide when a grey mist descends on the pasture,
The boy wends his homeward way with the animal quietly following.

6. Unimpeded

On the verdant field the beast contentedly lies idling his time away,

No whip is needed now, nor any kind of restraint;

The boy too sits leisurely under the pine tree,
Playing a tune of peace, overflowing with joy.

The Unorthodox Ox

7. Laissez Faire

The spring stream in the evening sun flows languidly along the willow-lined bank,

In the hazy atmosphere the meadow grass is seen growing thick; When hungry he grazes, when thirsty he quaffs, as time sweetly slides,

While the boy on the rock dozes for hours not noticing anything that goes on about him.

8. All Forgotten

The beast all in white now is surrounded by the white clouds,
The man is perfectly at his ease and carefree, so is his companion;

The white clouds penetrated by the moonlight cast their white shadows below,

The white clouds and the bright moonlight each following its course of movement.

The Unorthodox Ox

9. The Solitary Moon

Nowhere is the beast, and the oxherder is master of his time,

He is a solitary cloud drifting lightly along the mountain peaks;

Clapping his hands he sings joyfully in the moonlight,
But remember a last wall is still left barring his homeward walk.

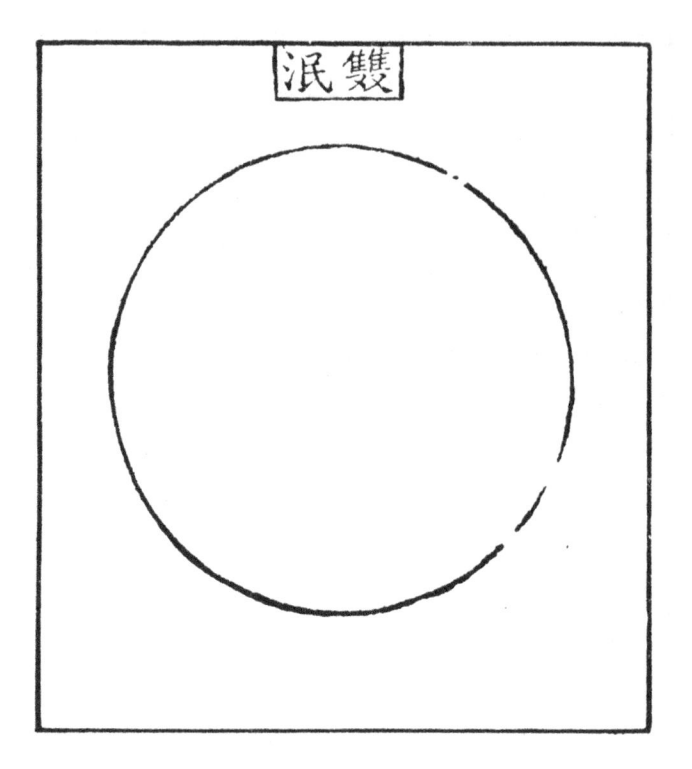

10. Both Vanished

Both the man and the animal have disappeared, no traces are left,

The bright moonlight is empty and shadowless with all the ten-thousand objects in it;

If anyone should ask the meaning of this,
Behold the lilies of the field and its fresh sweet-scented verdure.

— Kaku-an Shi-en

The Unorthodox Ox

But where has the master and his ox gone to? Is a question to ask while being able to entertain a favourite pastime, which is to entertain associating ruminations inside an open mind that is swelling beyond the limits of its own endless limitations, having left the plot altogether behind.

The real dimension was holding barely.

§

In the time they had before they were to leave on her tour she prepared the repertoire that she was to perform for her season. He had entertained himself with algorithms, playing with fractals and formulas that he was pulling apart and putting back together in another order, being attentive to not leave behind any symbols or numbers to worry about.

Then it was after the last of the vegetables that had been harvested. They ploughed the garden under and they closed her house for the winter. They left on her tour.

Starting off in western Europe they headed north and eastward. From Wales travelling to Scotland and England, they went on to Holland, Belgium, Denmark, France, and Germany. She performed varied programs. French music for the French, German composers for the Germans, and continental music for the English.

Then it was during the days when she was rehearsing with orchestras, ensembles, and accompanists, that he went out to look at the sights. He walked through museums and strolled in parks and there were occasions when he spoke with strangers, whenever he was called upon to do so, and he answered inquiries that he did not always know the answers to that a passerby might have asked him about. At the end of the day they met and discussed matters while of interest. That was the routine.

They went east through East Germany, on to Poland, to Russia, Moscow, where as far eastward as they were to go they stayed for a longer period.

There she played with her Russian friends who were still long-suffering from a tradition of willful sacrifice that had always been relied upon since the introduction of Christianity and from when the Cossacks had begun to ride or since the arrival of the first man and woman upon the steppes.

The Russian audiences applauded her performances for the expression and clarity of tone and flawless intonation, for the rhythms and the voicings that spoke to them of how they had endured.

From the east going back towards the west.

They travelled back through Poland, Slovakia, on to Hungary, to Budapest where she was engaged to perform with the Hungarian National Philharmonic, and she was to perform a recital with a French Canadian pianist in the National Concert Hall.

But in the streets of Budapest citizens were marching against the state of affairs; they were protesting and demanding for their voices to be heard, but not in any way for what they might have wanted to necessarily say in their heart of hearts or speak intimately about.

There were security measures, armed police and soldiers were out to restore the established order in the city.

Yet it was in spite of the unsettled state of unrest, Mary-Adeline was to honour her engagements. She had made an undeterred decision not to accept how the unpredictable disturbances might interfere. She would perform and was not to be dissuaded.

So it was on the day when she was rehearsing that he went out and joined in with the crowds. There was trouble. As required the security forces dealt with the crowds firing control munitions to disperse the mobs that ran away in a panic, and with so many others he stampeded away to escape the riot and it was with a faction that had splintered off on its own recognizance, he was following along with everyone, heading off into a adjacent park and out and over an expansive lawn, going in a direction that offered hope for escape, but not ultimate salvation. The pursued protesters went through the park under the branches of leafless trees. Dry fountains were full of dead leaves. And out the other end of the public space and out into a web of side streets, those who had made it out and had not imagined that they could have disappeared into the bushes fanned out into different directions. What was desperate shouting faded away.

He was somewhere else then at a juncture, where he had stopped to get his bearings. He was standing at the end of a deserted street. He was inside a small village inside the larger city. Narrow alleyways led in and out of the village, and down an inclined medieval lane were facing rows of diminutive houses that were low in height for the shorter people who had lived in them when originally built. Then drawing attention to the threshold of the houses were painted doors in bright colours: red, yellow, green, violet, orange, and blue. The welcoming doors had shiny polished brass door knockers.

While he was standing and looking down the lane, there was no one going in or coming out of the coloured doors. No one was coming along to make use of the brass door knockers and to knock at the luminously painted entrances and to be welcomed into the peace and quiet of a family's ancient ancestral home.

He was lost, but safe and sound.

On a corner was a church. The doors to it were also closed. Off to one side there was an outdoor terrace with tables and chairs in front of it. At a table seated was an elderly woman. She saw he was lost and she called him over to ask if she could give him the directions he needed. The woman's kindness was exemplary. He accepted the help offered. He was gracious in thanking her.

Then on the table in front of the old woman, there was a pot of tea. Perhaps he would like to join her? She asked. It was a fresh pot of tea she said. He was thirsty from running. Yes.

The woman when introducing herself and shaking his hand assured him and promised him that there was no need to worry about the dark colour of her hands. It was ingrained colouring in her skin because of her occupation. It was not filth that would rub off on him. She told him she was a potter and a sculptor. She was an artisan of the craft of the black ceramics of Nádudvar. She said she imagined that it would have been unlikely that he had heard of the ceramics of Nádudvar. That was understandable. He had not. She was composed, easy-going, systematic and methodical, and so she provided information on her profession, as to how the black clay was extracted from the earth, on the working of it, how the glazing and firing was done, what the uses for the ceramics were, she spoke about. Then she hinted that he couldn't have been at all interested to know as much about it as he pretended. Maybe not. But she acknowledged that it was not a problem not to be interested in the black ceramics from the great plain region of Hungry. The teapot before her she pointed out was an example of what the fuss was about. The large black pot due to its size she struggled with to pour him a cup of tea. She refused his offer for assistance in lifting it.

The woman was old enough to have been suffering from the afflictions that the old suffer from: aches and pains, memory loss, grim thoughts on mortality.

She told him that she had lived years abroad during the previous struggles. The common language she spoke well. She was engaging to converse with and so as they were talking, hardly as strangers, they got on to discussing the relevant matter of oxherding and what it is to be freed or to be tamed or trained, and how that related to a state of growing disquiet and unease in all of Hungry and in the wide world, and they had said as much as they were going to. So it was time for him to head off. Then that was when she asked him if the pottery she had to sell might be of interest to him. Her studio was across the street. It would be easy for him to have a look. That had been her plan.

He looked over and examined the woman's collection of black teapots, mugs, cups and saucers, sets of plates, and original creations, and so after enough deliberation and polite encouragement from the seller he bought a statue of a glazed black Buddha.

He thanked her for the tea, the conversation, the Buddha, and the directions.

The police forces in the streets were celebrating their victory. Harold went along his way holding on to a symbol of love, peace, and wisdom, tucked under his arm.

At the hotel restaurant Mary-Adeline was waiting for him. A noticeable spot of blood on his shirt got her attention.

— It is not mine, someone else's. He is going to be all right, I hope, he said.

— You weren't hurt?

— I sustained a few bruises, nothing serious. So I was delayed to buy you a present to compensate for being late.

He gave her the Buddha that was wrapped in paper.

— I need something to drink.

He poured himself a glass of wine from a bottle that was on the table.

— I'll tell you what it is, a Buddha, and here we are in Budapest. She unwrapped it.

— It's a laughing Buddha, she said.

The Unorthodox Ox

— He can take the place of your statue of Lenin. And there are no statues of Lenin having a good laugh. There's documentation and it says it's authentic. But what else could it be?

He got out the receipt and gave it to her.

— For two thousand two hundred and fifty forints we have an authentic Buddha and with its inscription.

She read out the inscription on the base of the statue.

— *When it comes to matters of religion, most persons prefer chewing the menu to actually eating the food.*

He sipped the wine.

— Which brings to mind an unrelated Chinese proverb. *A peasant can wait for a long time with an open mouth before a cooked duck flies into it*, he said.

— He can't take the place of my statue of Lenin, she said.

— It has to be better to worship a fat Asian than a skinny Slav. Then his presence will enlighten us and get us onto the righteous path towards enlightenment, the fast-track to enlightenment.

— We'd want to take our time. No?

— You're right, then hoping for slow enlightenment to appreciate the journey up into the firmament, if that is where enlightenment occurs, in the bright firmament.

— We're in no hurry.

— We can take our time.

— Although regarding your reference to the firmament, I can't make a pronouncement on that.

— Then we shall try to watch the days go by as a slow and enlightening process. The other possibility is that it will creep up on us and catch us by surprise, scare us out of our wits and we'll head for the hills. The wine is good.

She rubbed the Buddha's belly for good fortune.

— But stop me Mary-Adeline, don't let me overindulge. Because I might be tempted to experience a satori. After today's events I could be tempted. Then sudden enlightenment and we wouldn't be able to say why or how it occurred.

They drank the wine and ate salty goulash when it arrived.

They were watching people go by on a walkway by the Danube River in the moonlight that was shining on calm waters.

Then there was a unique effect in the air of unintelligible

whispering in a Finno-Ugrian language. They heard the sound of a gypsy violinist.

When they finished their meal they went out to walk with the crowds by the river. Mary-Adeline dropped money into the violinist's case.

Then under a lamplight, up into the light, he held the black Buddha. The moon was overhead.

— This fat pacifist, Buddha, he said.

— He's not too attractive.

— Shall we throw it into the Danube and watch it sink to the depths or float away?

— No, I'll keep it.

— Despite his appearance?

— Not only for that reason.

— He reminds me of someone I met once.

They went along by the river before turning around. The music of the violinist faded out. People were heading home.

— It's peaceful, she said.

— Something has happened.

— It seems so.

— There's the moon shining over Budapest. There are boats on the water, and these freedom-loving Hungarians. I felt young again, like there was something to fight for. God, I felt like an idealist when the police were hunting us down. So a lot has to be still possible. Maybe that's why I bought a Buddha, and we talked, the sculptress and I. It was an unusual conversation. We talked about one thing and were saying something else. How funny it is when events occur for their own sake, but that is always the case in fact.

They walked back to their hotel.

They were getting ready to go to sleep, and she asked him a question.

— It would be difficult to imagine what it would be like never to have hoped for anything, he answered.

— That's not quite what I meant, and I am not sure what I meant, she said and laughed to excuse their confusion.

— I didn't understand?

— It's my fault.

— Or mine.

The Unorthodox Ox

— Our fault.

— I do want to understand if possible.

— What I meant, I don't know myself. I am making it impossible for you.

— More interesting.

— That's always the case?

— I wish I knew how it was possible to love someone so much.

— I don't know either.

— You don't?

— Not exactly.

— How amazing that is then.

— Are you tired?

— I should be, from running and from my high hopes running away on me.

— I too am tired.

They spoke some more and not at length.

§

He was sitting at the hotel room's desk on which the statue of Buddha was resting. He took up a sheet of the hotel stationery, and he wrote out a note, a message that he addressed to possible recipients, c.c.: Mary-Adeline, Isa, Trudi, Elrod, Henri Lai, and to unknown readers. He wrote: *we know how enlightenment is unreachable even when in love, so we have had no choice but to arrive at the fateful conclusion that any opportunity for improvement that will lead to change will be overlooked, just when the conditions that will lead to the need for it are critical, then the worst of what's to be will be happening and when it does, a number of defeats will accumulate and the realization of the worsening state of affairs will exhibit itself manifestly and what is unavoidable will become inevitable and whatever previous accomplishments there were will never happen again. Progress will stop and cease to advance. A step forward will be followed by several in the opposite direction until the only direction in which to move is backwards, so far back there will be no hope for the smallest step forward. The age of defeat will come arriving as expected on the eve and on the hour of the last battle. Orders will be given for ultimate sacrifice, but it will be too late. None will be left to be made on the eve, on the hour, of the last last battle. Moans of despair will fall on our deaf ears. Our cries for mercy will be unanswered. But what am I saying? Forgive me. It's this dread that hangs over us. We see where people have been slaughtering each other for centuries and now what? But there is music to listen to, a few good stories worth telling, pictures to look at, and a few laughs to enjoy, good food to eat, someone to love, friends, and other excuses not to become overwrought.*

Anyway, I'm alive,

He signed his note with what would have been a pseudonym for another man like himself.

§

They travelled on to Prague where in the centre of the city on display were statues of forgotten saints and long dead kings looking upwards towards the heavens or they were bowing their heads down in shame or vacantly looking out into space. The living inhabitants were going about with what was a similar outlook on the future.

Then on that day a film was being shot in the old town. It was an epic judging by the decor. And there was a crowd of extras, they were following instructions to live in mortal fear for their lives. They had to cower and get down onto their knees and hold a position as a rebel walked amongst them. A tragic/comic actor was throwing his hat up into the air as an empty gesture. It took a number of takes to get right. The light was changing moment to moment unfavourably. The main protagonists of the film were not present on the set to help inspire the cast of extras to dig within themselves and understand the seriousness of the dire moment. It was a joke. The dour Czechs had a good time of it, as much as they were able to.

— The food in this country says a lot about how people are, Mary-Adeline said.

Her afternoon rehearsal with the Ceská Filharmonie had been difficult. Members of the wind section had been inebriated and had played too loudly.

So it was late that night, in their hotel room, he opened up a message that in the subject line read. Re: *Your estranged wife.* The message from a close family acquaintance said: *I am to inform you that your estranged wife has died.*

There was an attached copy of the newspaper obituary that listed the names of related and extended family members and there was the date, place, and the time for the services.

— What now? Why? I ask. But really, I imagine that this is what can happen when anything is possible. And it doesn't matter why, how, who, what or when. But I don't know how to respond. I don't know how to react, what my response should be.

Mary-Adeline was rubbing the Buddha's belly and removed her hand.

— The obituary doesn't give much information. Then I should be thankful it doesn't say, 'She's survived by her estranged husband.' That wouldn't be included. They wouldn't mention that the deceased wife is, 'Survived by her poor estranged husband.' They wouldn't include that. It doesn't say she died of a broken heart either. It says nothing. She's gone for no reason whatsoever and that seems to be it.

He made a call to confirm the news and to find out what he could.

— An accident, then I guess anything can happen to anyone at any time for no reason at all. But I don't want to imagine that if it weren't for us, because of us. So I do not want to go back for the funeral. I will have to. Then I can't be held responsible, can I? But why is it impossible to be a good person? Why is it difficult not to betray others? Those closest to us are harmed by each other. And our only hope for anything comes down to one formula:

$$P_E(H) = [P(H)/P(E)] \, P_H(E)$$

— What is that? she asked.

— It can be a formula for success, and it also works for failure. We can at least know what our odds are. I have to believe she did not accidentally take her own life or almost willingly did so.

— It wasn't that?

— Accidents can be interpreted in different ways. But I ought to take this seriously, her senseless death. Then at the funeral I'll cry, beat my chest with my fists, gnash my teeth. What will I do? What am I going to do at her funeral?

— You'll be stoic.

— I know how to be stoic. I do.

He removed her shoes and socks for her.

— I can't be expected to think nothing of it. But she was an impossible human being. Then I will have to forgive her some day. Now would be a good time.

— You've already done so.

— I tried. But what next? What now?

She gave him an affectionate kick to get his undivided attention that he gave to her.

§

From out the window of the plane he was watching the slow gradual fading of the evening, due to the direction in which the plane was flying.

He was home, back home. At customs he had forgotten to declare the Buddha. It was confiscated.

He was driving in the country. Along the sides of the roads drifts were piled up. Stubble was sticking up out of the snow in the fields.

On his way he stopped at a café to eat, and the woman who served him seemed to have recognized him. It had been a long time they both said. They didn't know how long. Neither remembered how long. They asked what had become of one another.

The waitress said that she had got married, then she had been taking care of her husband who was symptomatically ill from an undiagnosed nervous disorder. She was working for the both of them at two jobs, but "her man" day by day was getting better, she hoped.

He mentioned how he might say something about what he had been doing for so many years.

— But it doesn't matter, as nothing is as we expect, even when we escape from what we dread the most. Because what is there to escape from and come back to or back for? Death. We come back to death, for death. My estranged wife has just died and I've come back for her funeral, you see.

She asked him a question and they realized that they had mistaken the other for someone else.

— I'm sorry for your loss.

— Thank you, no one else will be.

The Unorthodox Ox

He left a generous tip.

He had a night to rest before the services. A loud wind kept him up.

§

Family, friends, and colleagues were sharing in laughter and in their tears. Mothers and fathers were weeping for the child of someone else. The details about the tragedy no one was to directly speak about. That was not what was important.

There were those who addressed him as the bereaved widower who were sympathetic. They could not have known about his situation. Others were to avoid him, not knowing what to say out of confusion, embarrassment, or anger. But there was then an older woman, an overweight lady, who knew of his shenanigans, and the woman believed that she had the right to speak her mind. When the funeral service ended she waddled up to him and she said.

— You're a despicable man. You're an abomination. Do you know that?

— I might be, in fact.

— You think you are clever, I bet.

— No, I am stoic.

— How her mother must feel.

— Excuse me, I would rather avoid unpleasantness at this time.

— You're an immoral man.

— You have made your point, thank you.

— You are being glib. I get it. Oh, you're clever, a real smart-ass. You must think you are smart.

— I don't know you, lady, and maybe what you're saying is interesting, though not convincing, because do you know anything? You don't, and I suspect you're an example of that type of ignorant windbag who will believe anything, but knows nothing, and like others of your kind is foolish enough to think you know something about everything but you know nothing about anything, and so it's a question of self-righteousness when it comes to that. Then you're arrogant enough to think you have reason to be insulted and indignant and that someone would want to go to the trouble to acknowledge even abstractly that such well thought out beliefs are carved in stone.

— What did you say to me?

The woman's husband had come along to lead her away. He pleaded with her not to make a scene, but it was too late. The fat lady had sung her song. She stomped off.

He was moved to tears.

Then in attendance there was his friend with whom he had spoken to from the hotel suite.

— You're crying? What is wrong with you, Harold?

— I'm all right. I'm drying my tears is all.

— You know, you're better off. Divorce can ruin a person. That joke about: why is divorce so expensive? Because it's worth it. It is true, but it's not amusing. And I won't have anything left when my divorce is decided. My children are turning against me. You're lucky you don't have children.

— We weren't ready for that.

— It's too late now.

— I'm afraid so.

— You can laugh already?

— No, not yet.

— But you know, it's funny, I admit I miss my wife sometimes. It is odd how I miss her. I miss the contempt she showed me that I mistook for her love and affection. But if this were my funeral she would be here dancing on my grave, laughing until she cried. So then how has the trip been?

— Enlightening.

— Well, let us keep in touch. You can let me know how well things are going for you, and the way she died. I am sure I will go myself in a similar way, doing something I'd regret. My condolences I give you.

A strong north wind was blowing. The cold burial was short-lived. No one was to stay on to linger sadly by the grave-side.

Then the day's passing was uplifting and depressing. Emotional highs and lows came and went.

That evening the temperature dropped further. A stronger wind came up. He stayed home. He did not attend what was a memorial party. No one had invited him.

Then the following day he spoke with Isa, and she was to update him on what was turning out to be the making of a legacy around his name. So she had to have thought that he would have been interested to know that his replacement was not filling his shoes, but that would have been impossible for another mere mortal, she said.

She in the meantime had fallen in love with a man who was infertile.

— If only everything wasn't so complicated all the time, she said to him.

Then if he could still help her out, she would be grateful to him, she promised.

— No, I just buried my ex-wife for Christ's sake.

But what day could be better than the day after he had buried his ex-wife to father a child with another woman to make up for his loss? She teased him.

— It's too much to think about, he said.

— Of course it is. I only wanted to ask and I'll keep asking until I'm barren.

They agreed to come to the same understanding and left things as they were.

§

Then the last of his possessions that he had left behind, he had arranged to retrieve, and so Helen was waiting for him to come by. They had spoken briefly at the funeral.

In the yard, there was a "For Sale" sign that explained the chaotic disarray inside.

— I've been assured the house will sell quickly, Helen said to him as he went in.

— It ought to, he said.

— Excuse the mess.

— It's all right. I was used to it.

— I've had to do a lot of organizing, which is helping me to keep busy.

— Then how are you doing, Helen?

— I'm not sure. Then did you know the roost box you put out

for bluebirds has been occupied?
— Has it?
— Karol was putting out meal-worms and insect suit, as you instructed, but meal-worms are expensive and are hard to come by at this time of year. She was getting crickets for them when available.
— They like crickets.
— I appreciate the plumage of the males.

She led him to the back window to see if there were bluebirds.
— It doesn't look like they are out now, she said.
— They wouldn't be. This isn't their usual feeding time.
— You know what you have come to get? she asked.
— Yes.

The axe was in the stump where he had left it, the handle was sticking up through the snow.
— So this is going to be hard, but I imagine we get used to everything eventually. And I had a friend, she took a year to mourn after her boy died. Then she went on as before. I'll go on, but not as before. I don't see how I could. And I keep asking myself why I wasn't able to teach her to want less of everything. I don't know how I could have done that. It is hard to teach a child to want less and do more while wanting less. When she was born I thought we would know each other for a long time.

He had to go.
— You've everything you came for? she asked.
— I think so.
— Well, I hope you will visit me sometime whenever you want.
— I will visit. I will.
— When you come back maybe.
— Yes.
— You'd be welcome.
— Thank you.
— I am going to feel sad for such a long time, I know. You've everything?
— I'll come back if I haven't.
— I'd like you to.
— I will.
— Then Harold, you know, I think I'm afraid that I am going to become one of those women who doesn't listen to anyone, who

The Unorthodox Ox

talks to herself, who is angry all the time. I am worried about being alone with no one to talk to. I'll become eccentric for all the wrong reasons. And I'll sit around and try to figure out where I've misplaced my days. They are gone.

— But you have what you remember. There's always that.

— In the end our days are gone.

— Though there's always tomorrow, he said unconvincely.

— There is not always tomorrow. And I'm going to be waiting to forget everything.

She kissed him on either cheek and asked him again to visit her when he was around. He promised he would. She didn't believe him, but would forgive him that.

— You shouldn't say so, she said.

— I'll surprise you.

— Surprise me, I'd like that.

His ex-mother-in-law he would never see again, as she did not have long to live.

§

He stored his insect display cases and other belongings in an assigned spot.

Then he went outside and he walked out into his old footsteps, past the empty church plot, the filled-in graves and the houses of the town. He walked out into the familiar field and trudged out onto a layer of wind-blown snow. He went down to the river. It was frozen along the edges. He stood there for a while until his extremities were stiff from the cold.

Later back at Mary-Adeline's, he remembered what it was that he wanted to remember and also account for in some way and he got out from the stored boxes his letters, reports, and notes, written in his particular style, similar to his words to what they were in that same old drone.

So there was the one memo that he had been looking for that as he read it was the same as he remembered.

I am again experiencing a hatred for what I have to do, and I'll have to see what I can put up with and if I can't manage it I'll have to see regardless. But how annoying it is that I've found myself to be in a situation as to how I always imagined hell, but it's only for a few more weeks, months, years, an entire lifetime. Unless by some miracle I were to fall in love and live happily ever after and there is this possibility, maybe not a fantasy in which I would be capable of more than I suspect myself capable of, of love and life and communion with someone who would be happy to anoint me. So how curious it was, today, sometime today, I was tempted to go back to bed and dream, but then I got on with my work to put a few thoughts together and to express myself and had anyone been around I'd have shared my thoughts, but as no one was anywhere to be seen I kept them to myself and I thought back to when nothing meant too much, which permitted me to resume my day's work. My work, that is or should be to investigate what is forever hidebound.

But be careful, watch out you bounder, you numbskull, you nincompoop, you need to be careful when imagining who thinks who is talking to whom.

Love and with sincere regret,
Your conscience

So perhaps his conscience had wanted to speak out on behalf of what is right and wrong, but as an unreliable guide he had been unable to distinguish between the two and so he had come to rely upon every excuse in the book and he would maybe have reached the conclusion that morally one shouldn't have cared to begin with or couldn't afford to.

But what had he been thinking and wondering about? What could have been so trying that a pang of conscience would have felt compelled to lay so terrible as was his heartache at his symbolically anointed feet that through the years had almost caused him to bleed to death in a dream?

So then his folder of suicide notes he leafed through, and he laughed at the seriousness of their failed intent. He laughed at the loss of Buddha and enlightenment, for the loss of everything.

Then he was sitting beside the statue of Lenin in front of a fire that he had made, and he burned his letters of resignation and suicide notes. If only those flames had been eternal.

Later going back outside he stood in one place and he looked up into the night at the stars and resolved himself half-heartedly to become in some way immortal for not having had a good reason to live.

Click

And it was in Dresden, in the rebuilt part of the city, Mary-Adeline the night before had cooked a seven-course meal for the members of two competing world-renowned string quartets. The food had been delicious, the talk civilized until the subject of interpretation came up, and all hell broke loose.

Then maybe with all things equal, nothing happened from one moment to the next, as it happens when change is not what we measure with time, but time is what we measure with changes.

Click

As for the other, that negative faded away.

Click

Snow was falling in light flakes and clinging to the branches of the apple trees. Smoke from the chimney in wisps rose up. The night was getting colder. It was late. Too late to have gone for a walk in the snow-fields.

Click

But it was not too late to stay up and listen to requiems from her collection of medieval, classical, baroque, romantic, and modern contemporary requiems. Long slow death-inspired lamentations. He hummed along with the pieces he knew and listened carefully to the contemporary work that needed to be listened to—to be understood and appreciated for the discordant prophecies therein and he did appreciate them.

Click

He listened to requiems throughout the night and on other nights and for the rest of what was a lifetime he opened his ears to requiems that were not a part of the repertoire of the woman he loved and was to go on worshipping and they were not joyful requiems. No. They were the large important and dramatic requiems of loss and endless sorrow, full of sombre cellos and double basses and bellowing ox-like wind instruments and choruses of voices calling out for a shred of forgiveness.

Then that other negative into a bottomless hole kept fading away, yet he was to continue speaking out on behalf of unqualified statements and for the noise of others or for the sound of a moment's silence, so asking for peace, begging for it, when and if confronting complaints that can be made while enduring an endless process of relentless self-discipline, which can remove happiness from spontaneous moments of celebration.

Then backing up and going back to the first glimmer, not to just the thought of a glimmer, but of the notion of a glimmer, a hint of one, to an impossible explanation of what the original glimmer was: nothing, something, that was strange and that was rooted into nothing or everything.

§

As for the trip to Madagascar, why not? For a great lepidopterological journey from which to never return.

Who was talking? Who now? Was talking? Saying what exactly and to whom?

— It's no different for anyone else what we have to put up with.
— It is not.
— And if I were to run off and kill myself why not someone like you or someone like anyone?
— Apart from myself you're not the only man who would say so. But what of one's sense of honour? I do not want to believe in having to be dishonourable.
— You don't.
— Given what I owe you.
— You are for me completely forgiven.
— You think I'm mad, but you yourself are not sane.
— I don't pretend to be.
— Pretense is sanity? What can be proven with such an argument?
— What do you want to know about what we have to prove?
— Nothing at all.

Who was talking?

Click.

Then it is finally possible to doubt claims about trying to make a statement one way or another and to go on further and challenge the idea that there is another claim that would come along and still to go further and challenge that something has happened since the beginning or thereafter.

So that night the applause was loud and long for Mary-Adeline's performance. The audience had requested encores. She had played several and the crowd had shouted and howled out their appreciation for the experience to last.

Afterwards a group of friends took her out to celebrate, and she was then told about someone she knew who had died, a young musician, a new talent. Someone who had been blessed, a terrible waste. There is always someone who is not meant to live.

Then there was amongst her friends an old lover of hers, who asked if he could accompany her back to her hotel. He insisted she not go alone. It was late, dark, and dangerous. She fought him off. She won. She always won.

Who was fighting?

Click.

— Everything's all right here. There's not much snow on the ground. It's blown away, Harold said to her.

— It's cold? Mary-Adeline asked.

— Yes, and I went for a walk yesterday. It was so cold I didn't think I was going to make it back home alive.

— I too am in mourning for someone I knew who has died.

— This has to stop.

Who?

Click.

Who was talking? Who was trying to say one last parting word?

EPILOGUE

A RELATED LAST FUNERAL

A solitary individual man, who had been living in a house, at the end of a road. It had a ditch along the side of it. In the ditch his dogs ran from one end to the other. He had kept to himself. He did not visit others. Rarely he received visitors.

Every day he sat in front of his house looking down his road watching his dogs running in the ditch and that was all. Nothing happened, though from time to time he looked at his watch to see what time it was. But that was not important, because it appeared as if time would take its course.

So for weeks, months, and years, nothing happened until the one day when he heard what was not a precisely recognizable sound, and to find out what it was he went out to the main road where he found a wooden box, and to answer his curiosity for what was in the box, he kicked it, and there was the dull ringing sound of a bell that rang out. His dogs barked and howled. There was a commotion. Then there was a woman and an old man who appeared, coming out from a shadow cast in the dark, but from really nowhere. The woman was terrified, frightened, she was looking around and behind her back. She said.

"We have heard that before. It scared us then and frightens us now." The old man's lips and tongue were moving unintelligibly. He was a deaf-mute.

And the old couple then vanished away into the recently forgotten past.

So everything could have been the same as before, except for a feeling of bewilderment that he was experiencing and something was happening and he sat down on the box that he had kicked and he had to have been crying for a sad life that had failed to live up to the lowest of his expectations. His dogs licked him. They wagged their tails. He was not to be comforted, and so he would have had to have given up on what would have been an irresolvable conjectural hypothesis, but a truck drove up then and a man stepped out of it. The visitor introduced himself and said.

"That box you're sitting on fell off the back of my truck when I went by before. Then did an old man and woman come along? They might have said they remembered what they had heard once, and they were afraid for their lives. That 'ringing sound', some like to hear it, others do not and are afraid. A deaf-mute can tell us who does and who does not like the sound of it."

The visitor shook the box. The bell inside of it rang out.

"But for whom does it toll now? Then where is a deaf-mute when needed to tell us what we want to hear? I suspect he's lost in his silence and he is tormented, he's distressed, depressed, and troubled emotionally since the terrible accident."

And the solitary man understood some of what he had heard, and that is maybe why he opened up his feelings and he shared with the visitor how he remembered better days when he was younger, how he had spent his childhood growing up in the family bakery, what the smell of freshly baked bread was like to wake up to. He spoke about his time in school, how he had played the trumpet and had dreamed of one day playing and singing his heart out and after that.

There were the many years after that. The long days he had spent looking down his road at his dogs in the ditch. The years of being alone.

The men talked into the night. The dogs fell asleep. The two became friends and the man who was unsure of so much said he had never felt as if there had ever been a lot of anything to say.

Then the bell-man had to have suspected and known that that was the cue. It was time to leave. He loaded the box onto his truck.

"I'm transporting this bell that is for the ringing home of the dead. It is a funeral bell that keeps evil spirits away and from taking possession of a man's soul when moving into the next world, that is why we ring funeral bells. Well, it was nice to have met and to have talked. You have some nice dogs. So now then don't despair."

He drove away.

The man in doubt was happier from then on. He sold his house in the country and stopped living alone. He bought another house in the city. He married a woman who was recognized for her kindness, her intelligence, and her love. He and his wife had children and they opened a business that did well helping people who needed advice, and so they were to have saved a part of the world that they lived in and that was a lot of saving for what it was.

Then years later, on a beautiful sunny day, not a cloud in the sky, he said goodbye to his wife, children, and friends, and he died.

Made in the USA
Middletown, DE
29 August 2019